DISCARDED

"Is he asleep already?" Sara asked as Cole dropped onto his easy chair later that evening.

"Oh, yeah. After you finished his story and left the room, I only read as far as the third page of his second book before he closed his eyes. He had a busy day today."

"I'll say," she replied. "Building a snow family is hard work." The Baby Snowman had been Brody-sized and without adornment, until Brody had shaken his head and demanded a cap "like Daddy's."

Fortunately when Cole had named the family—Daddy, Mama and Baby—Brody hadn't objected. He'd posed happily beside *his* snowman for one of the many photos that Sara had taken.

To Sara's further delight he'd joined her in making snow angels, and had even gone so far as to grab her hand and tell her "more" when he wanted her to help him cover the yard with them.

Maybe she *was* making progress…

THE CHILD WHO RESCUED CHRISTMAS

BY
JESSICA MATTHEWS

Dedication:
To my family, especially my husband,
whose support never wavers.

All the characters in this book have no existence outside
the imagination of the author, and have no relation
whatsoever to anyone bearing the same name or names.
They are not even distantly inspired by any individual
known or unknown to the author, and all the incidents
are pure invention.

All Rights Reserved including the right of reproduction
in whole or in part in any form. This edition is published
by arrangement with Harlequin Enterprises II BV/S.à.r.l.
The text of this publication or any part thereof may
not be reproduced or transmitted in any form or by
any means, electronic or mechanical, including
photocopying, recording, storage in an information
retrieval system, or otherwise, without the written
permission of the publisher.

First published in Great Britain 2011
by Mills & Boon, an imprint of Harlequin (UK) Limited.
Large Print edition 2012
Harlequin (UK) Limited, Eton House,
18-24 Paradise Road, Richmond, Surrey TW9 1SR

© Jessica Matthews 2011

ISBN: 978 0 263 22446 7

Harlequin (UK) policy is to use papers that are
natural, renewable and recyclable products and made
from wood grown in sustainable forests. The logging
and manufacturing process conform to the legal
environmental regulations of the country of origin.

Printed and bound in Great Britain
by CPI Antony Rowe, Chippenham, Wiltshire

Jessica Matthews's interest in medicine began at a young age, and she nourished it with medical stories and hospital-based television programmes. After a stint as a teenage candy-striper, she pursued a career as a clinical laboratory scientist. When not writing or on duty, she fills her day with countless family and school-related activities. Jessica lives in the central United States, with her husband, daughter and son.

Recent titles by the same author:

MAVERICK IN THE ER
SIX-WEEK MARRIAGE MIRACLE
EMERGENCY: PARENTS NEEDED
HIS BABY BOMBSHELL
THE BABY DOCTOR'S BRIDE

These books are also available in eBook format from www.millsandboon.co.uk

Dear Reader

Have you ever made a mistake that you bitterly regretted—to the point where you wish you could turn back time and make a better choice? My hero, Cole, had such a moment in his life, and it eventually came back to haunt him. Naturally I had to create a heroine strong enough to bear up under the pressure, and the following pages are the result. And what better time to set a story about love and forgiveness, goodwill and peace, than at Christmas?

So, as you take time to enjoy the season, I hope Sara and Cole's journey will touch your heart.

Happy reading!

Jessica

PROLOGUE

THIS day just kept getting better, Sara Wittman thought wryly as one of the morning headlines caught her eye.

Three people killed in medical helicopter crash.

She hated reading news like that—it was a horrible way to start her day—but morbid curiosity and a healthy dread drove her to read the few facts listed in the article.

En route from the University of Oklahoma Medical Center in Oklahoma City to Enid, the A-Star 350 helicopter went down in an open field thirty miles outside its destination for unknown reasons. The three people on board, pilot James Anderson of Dallas, Texas, Nurse Ruth Warren of Tulsa, Oklahoma, and Nurse Lilian Gomez of Norman, Oklahoma, died at the scene.

According to statements released by AirMed, the company that operates this flying medical service, the circumstances of the crash are still uncertain. The incident is under investigation

*by the Federal Aviation Administration and the
National Transportation Safety Board.*

As a nurse assigned to the medical-surgical
floor of Nolan Heights Hospital, she occasionally cared for a patient who had to be flown to
a tertiary care center for treatment and consequently had met the dedicated staff who flew
those missions. Although Nolan Heights used
a different company for their flying ambulance
service, the men and women who specialized in
providing that type of medicine were a special
breed who'd garnered her respect. These people
would be missed, not only by their families but
also by the medical community as a whole.

"You're looking rather glum this morning."
Cole, her husband of nearly three years, breezed
into the kitchen wearing dark slacks and a rust-
colored shirt—his usual attire for another busy
day in his medical practice. He bussed her on the
cheek before heading for the coffeemaker where
she'd already poured a cup of the French roast
she'd made strong enough to keep him running
all morning.

She savored his husbandly peck before rattling
the newspaper. "I was just reading about a medical helicopter crash in Oklahoma. Two nurses

and the pilot were killed on the way to collect a patient."

"That's too bad," he remarked as he sipped from his mug and slipped a slice of bread into the toaster. "No one we know, I hope."

"No," she said, "although one of the nurses is from your old stomping grounds."

"Tulsa?"

"For being gone most of the night because of a patient, you're remarkably sharp this morning," she teased.

"It's all done with smoke and mirrors," he answered with a grin that after one year of dating, two years of living together and three years of marriage still jump-started her pulse every time. "But in answer to your question, Tulsa is a relatively large city. I didn't know every kid in my grade, much less my entire school."

"I suppose it would be surprising if you knew Ruth Warren."

He visibly froze. "Ruth Warren?"

"Yeah," she confirmed. "It doesn't give her age, though." Then, because the news had obviously startled him, she asked, "Did you know a Ruth Warren?"

"The one I knew was a schoolteacher," he said

slowly, his gaze speculative. "High school biology. Now that I think about it, she'd always talked about going into nursing. Maybe she finally did."

"Then it could have been your friend."

"I doubt it. Even if she did make a career change, the Ruth I knew was scared of heights. She'd always joked about how she'd never get on an airplane."

"There must be two Ruth Warrens," she guessed. "Both names are common enough and her surname could be her married name."

"It's possible," he murmured thoughtfully.

"Regardless, I'm sure her family, and everyone else's, is devastated."

"Hmm."

"And when a tragedy like this happens close to Christmas, it has to be even more difficult to handle," she commented, imagining how the season would never again be the same for those left behind. In the blink of an eye for these families, the holiday had lost its inherent excitement.

"Hmm."

Sara recognized his preoccupied tone. Certain his mind was already racing ahead to concentrate on the day's hectic schedule, she said offhand-edly, "It's nice that we're closing the hospital at noon today."

"Yeah."

He was definitely not paying attention. "And Administration is doubling everyone's salaries."

"That's nice." Suddenly, his gaze landed on her. "What?"

"You weren't listening to me, were you?" she teased.

A sheepish expression appeared on his face. "Apparently not. Sorry."

"You're forgiven," she said lightly. "As long as you won't forget our annual anniversary get-away."

"I haven't," he assured her. "We have reservations for the weekend at the hotel in Bisbee, just as we decided, and we fly to Arizona on Thursday morning. It amazes me that you wanted to stay at that elevation and see snow when we'll be seeing plenty of it soon enough," he added in a mock grumble. "A sunny beach would have made more sense."

"We did the sunny beach last year," she pointed out. "This is different. Besides…" she gave him a sultry smile "…if we run into any of the resident ghosts that our hotel claims to have, we can bar ourselves in our room."

He grinned. "I vote we do that anyway."

As if on cue, Sara's watch beeped with her five-minute warning. Without looking at the time, she drained her mug and placed it in the sink. "Gotta run or I'll be late," she said as she stopped to give him a goodbye kiss.

He threaded an arm around her waist and pulled her close, his solid warmth comforting. "Do we have plans for this evening?"

She thought a minute. "No, why?"

The playful expression she recognized appeared on his face. "I predict I'm going to need a nap when I get home."

Ordinarily, the prospect would have thrilled her, but not today.

"Maybe we'll get lucky and make a baby tonight," he murmured with a feral smile and a seductive voice.

If only that were possible...

"We won't," she said flatly. "As of a few days ago, I'm not pregnant. It's the wrong time."

Her husband's appreciative gaze turned sympathetic. "Oh, honey. I'm sorry. Maybe next month."

Next month. It always came down to next

month. For the last year and a half, those words had become her mantra.

"Yeah, maybe." Avoiding his gaze, she tried to pull out of his embrace, but he'd obviously heard the disappointment in her voice because he didn't let her go.

"Hey." His hand against the side of her face was gently reassuring. "It'll happen. Just be patient."

After all this time, her account holding that particular virtue was overdrawn. "I'm tired of being patient, Cole. We should see a different specialist." She finally voiced what she'd been contemplating off and on for the last month. "Dr. Eller could refer us to—"

"Sara," he chided, "Josh Eller is the best ob-gyn man in this part of the country. You know that."

"Yes, but another doctor might have a different opinion. He might take a more aggressive approach."

"A different doctor might," he agreed, "but Josh hasn't steered us wrong so far. You've gotten pregnant once. It's only been nine months."

Sadly, she'd miscarried within days after she'd learned she'd been expecting. Had she not been concerned about what she'd thought was a lingering stomach flu virus, she'd never have gone to the doctor, and when she'd miscarried, she would have attributed it to just another horrible period.

"But nothing's happened since," she protested. We should—"

"Be patient. Your body needs time to heal."

"Yes, but—"

"Josh said we should allow ourselves a year and we're close to that," he reminded her. "Life hasn't been so bad with just the two of us, has it?"

While their relationship hadn't sailed along on completely smooth seas—there'd been a brief ten days when they'd gone their separate ways because she'd despaired of him ever proposing and giving her the family and home life she wanted—she couldn't complain. "No, but a baby is like the icing on the cake when two people love each other. It—"

He stopped her in midsentence. "A baby will come if and when he's supposed to. You have to trust that Josh knows what he's doing. If he says not to worry, then don't."

She'd wanted Cole to be as eager to grow their family as she was, and his attitude grated on her. Didn't he understand how much she wanted this? Didn't he see that each passing month chipped away at her confidence and self-esteem?

And yet she understood Cole's propensity to maintain the status quo when it came to his personal life. Although he never said, she guessed that losing his parents at such an early age and the subsequent turmoil in his life had made him reluctant to modify an established routine. She didn't necessarily like his behavior, but it was a part of his character and she accepted it.

"Look," she began, "I know how difficult it is for you to change course when you're happy with the path you're on. After all, between dating and living together, it took you almost three years before you finally proposed, but you should be as excited about a baby as I am."

"I am."

"You don't act like it," she mumbled.

He raised an eyebrow. "Would wringing my hands and calling Josh every week, pestering him for information and advice, change things?"

He had a point. "No," she conceded. "But I want you to want this as much as I do and I'm not getting that impression from you." While she knew Cole was more reserved than most, she wanted to see a more enthusiastic response. "Sometimes I think you only agreed to have a baby to humor me."

"Oh, Sara." He patted her back as he hugged her. "I'll admit that I'm not eager for our lives to change because I'm happy with just the two of us. But I'd be happy if you got pregnant, too. A little girl with your pixie nose would be cute. So, you see, I'm basically a happy kind of guy." He winked.

His teasing tone defused her aggravation. "Oh, you." She poked him playfully. "Pixie nose, indeed."

"Seriously, Sara…" his gaze grew intent "…stressing out about the situation won't help matters. Josh won't steer us wrong."

Her husband's confidence soothed her frazzled nerves. Slowly, she nodded. "You're right, he won't."

"Good girl." He cupped her face with both hands and kissed her. "There's no doubt in my mind that it'll happen, so stop worrying. Before long, you'll be complaining about morning sickness, swollen ankles and not being able to see your own feet."

She offered a wan smile. "I guess. Now, I'd better run or I really will be late."

After she'd left, bundled against the cold, Cole noticed how quiet the house seemed without his bubbly wife's presence. He'd hated seeing her so downcast for those few minutes and he wished Sara would focus on what she had rather than what she didn't have. She'd always made it plain that she wanted a large family—two boys and two girls—like the one she'd had growing up, and while the thought of being responsible for four children—*four*—was enough to scare him spitless, he'd been willing to patiently *and thoroughly* do his part to fulfill her dream. He grinned as he remembered the last time they'd made love. They'd started in the kitchen then detoured to their oversize soaker tub before ending up in bed.

He enjoyed nights like those—craved them, in fact—and he wasn't in any particular hurry to lose them. Truth was, he liked having his wife to himself. The idea that he someday would have even fewer private moments with her than he did now only made him cherish those times all the more.

While he looked upon their inability to conceive as one of the temporary mountains of life some people had to face—and was, in fact, a little relieved because he'd had so little experience with a loving family—she saw it as a personal failure. She shouldn't, of course, because they were only in the early stages of the process. She'd gotten pregnant within six months of when they'd stopped using any birth control and although she'd lost the baby, only another nine months had passed. Consequently, they'd never thought they'd needed fertility testing, although if nothing happened soon, they would.

And yet he truly did believe what he'd told her. Mother Nature simply needed time to work and Josh would decide on the proper time for medical science to intervene.

Content to leave the situation in his colleague's capable hands, he sat down to polish off his toast and coffee. As he munched, he idly glanced at the newspaper his wife had discarded and the trepidation he'd felt when Sara had first mentioned the helicopter crash came back, full force.

Ruth Warren.

Surely the woman wasn't the same Ruth Warren from his youth—the same Ruth Warren he'd spent time with a few years ago at his fifteen-year class reunion. The same class reunion when he'd drowned his sorrows with far too many margaritas because Sara had left him.

In spite of his reluctance to take the step she'd wanted—marriage—he'd come to his senses quickly. Accepting that his life would stretch ahead interminably without her, he'd proposed a week later. Sara had never pressed for details about his change of heart and he'd never offered them, except to say that he'd been miserable without her. Six months later, after Sara had planned her dream wedding, they had been married. Now, in a few more weeks, they'd celebrate their three-year anniversary.

Three years of the happiness and contentment he hadn't felt since he was eight.

Suddenly, he had to know if the Ruth Warren mentioned in the article was the girl who'd often sat beside him at school because their names fell so close alphabetically. Now that he thought about it, hadn't she mentioned during their reunion weekend that she'd turned her teaching certificate into a nurse's diploma? To be honest, there was a lot about those two days he didn't remember…

Determined to find an answer, he abandoned his coffee on his way to his office and powered up his computer. Minutes later, he'd found the online obituary at the *Tulsa World* website and scanned the details. Most, he already knew.

Age 33, preceded in death by her parents, at-

tended the University of Oklahoma, earned a degree in secondary education and later in nursing before taking a position as a flight nurse.

Reading the facts suddenly made them seem familiar, as if she'd told him of her career change and he'd simply forgotten. He read on…

Survivors include a son, as well as many friends and former students.

She'd had a son? She hadn't mentioned a child, but she'd never been one to share the details of her personal life. He was certain he'd asked about her life—it had been a reunion, after all—but he'd been too focused on his own misery to remember the things she'd told him. Idly, he wondered if the boy's father was still in the picture. Probably not, if the man hadn't received mention.

A graveside service will be held at 10:00 a.m. Wednesday at the Oaklawn Cemetery.

Cole leaned back in his chair and stared blankly at the screen. The description of Ruth's life had been rather succinct, and certainly didn't do justice to the young woman he remembered. She'd lived through a horrible childhood, carried enough baggage to fill a plane's cargo hold and had a gift for defusing tense moments with a wisecrack, but she'd always been a great listener.

And now Ruth was gone. Of course, he hadn't talked to her since that weekend, but now he wished he'd contacted her and told her that he'd taken her advice. He'd faced his demons and followed his heart. Now it was too late.

Then again, Ruth had probably known…

It was hard to believe that someone Cole's own age, someone who should have lived another fifty years or so, someone with whom Cole had grown up with, was gone. Her death gave him a glimpse of his own mortality, and suddenly he wished he'd taken off the entire week to spend with Sara instead of just two days.

For an instant, he toyed with the idea of attending Ruth's funeral, then decided against it. Depending on how old her son was, offering condolences would either be overwhelming or wouldn't mean anything at this point. It would be better if he wrote a letter for the boy to read when he was ready—a letter telling him what a wonderful friend his mother had been.

And although he knew Ruth would never have mentioned their one-night stand to anyone even in passing, in one tiny corner of his heart he was relieved that now it would remain a secret for all eternity.

CHAPTER ONE

"WHAT do you say you run away with me this weekend?" Sebastian Lancaster asked Sara two days later as she straightened his bedsheets during her last patient round before her shift-change report. "I know this great little place for dancing. I could show you a few steps that will make your head spin."

Sara smiled at her eighty-five-year-old patient who relied on a walker and wheezed with every breath, thanks to his years of habitual smoking. No doubt the only head that would spin with any sudden move would be his.

"No can do," she said cheerfully, already anticipating her upcoming weekend away from the daily grind of hospitals, patients and housework. "I already have plans."

"No problem." He coughed. "What is it they say? Plans are made to be broken."

"I think you're referring to rules, not plans," she corrected.

He waved a wrinkled, age-spotted hand. "Same difference. It's been ages since I've tangoed and if I'm not mistaken, you'd be good at it. Got the legs for it."

Knowing the elderly gentleman couldn't see past his elbow, she let his comment about her legs slide. "I'll bet you were quite the Fred Astaire in your day," she commented, giving the top blanket a final pat.

"Oh, I was. My wife and I could have outshone these young whippersnappers on those celebrity dance shows. So whaddya say? Wanna spring me from this joint so we can take a spin?"

She laughed at his suitably hopeful expression, although they both knew she couldn't fulfill his request. Between his emphysema and current bout of pneumonia, he was struggling to handle basic activities, much less add a strenuous activity like dancing. However, his physical limitations didn't stop this perpetual flirt from practicing his pickup lines. Sara guessed his wife must have been adept at keeping his behavior in check, or else she'd turned a blind eye to his Romeo attitude.

"Sorry, but I'm already running away this weekend," she told him, glancing at the drip rate of his IV. "With my husband, who just happens to be your doctor."

He nodded matter-of-factly, as if not particularly disappointed by his failure. "Shoulda known. The pretty ones are always taken. Must say, though…" he stopped to cough "…that if Doc had the good sense to pick you out of the eligible women, then he's got a good head on his shoulders."

"I like to think so," she said lightly, aware that her relationship with Cole had endured some dark days. However, in spite of the usual differences of opinion between people of diverse backgrounds and ideas, in spite of his initial reluctance to commit and in spite of her miscarriage nine months ago, life had been good.

"You two just going away for nothing better to do or for something special?"

"It's our three-year anniversary," she replied. "Actually, we still have a few weeks before the actual date, but this was the only weekend we could both get away."

"Ah, then you're still newlyweds. I'll bet you're eager to have your second honeymoon, even if it wasn't that long ago since your first, eh?" He cackled at his joke before ending on a cough.

Sara smiled. "It's always great to get away, honeymoon or not."

She'd been looking forward to this weekend for a month now and could hardly wait. Cole, on the other hand, had been preoccupied the last few days, which had been somewhat surprising because he'd been as eager to stay in the haunted historic hotel as she was.

"Too much to do before I can leave with an easy conscience," he'd said when she'd asked.

While that was probably true—as a hospitalist, he'd put in long hours to ensure the doctors covering his patients would find everything in order while he was gone—she had to wonder if something else wasn't on his mind. Still, she was confident that once they shook the dust of Nolan Heights off their feet, he'd leave those worries behind. And if distance didn't help, then the skimpy black lace negligee in her suitcase would.

"Well, go and have a good time," Sebastian said. "If he takes you dancing, dance a slow one for me." He winked one rheumy brown eye.

"I will," she promised. "When I come back to work on Monday, if you're still here, I'll tell you all about it."

"Do that," he said before he closed his eyes, clearly spent from their short conversation.

Sara strode out of the room, her soft soles silent on the linoleum. She'd begun to chart her final notes for her patients when another nurse, Millie Brennan, joined her.

"How's Mr. Lancaster this afternoon?"

Sara smiled at the twenty-six-year-old, somewhat jealous of her strawberry blond tresses when her own short hair was unremarkably brown. The only plus was that Sara's curls were natural whereas Millie's came from a bottle.

"As sassy as ever. Given his medical condition, it's amazing how he can still flirt with us."

"Wait until he feels better," Millie said darkly. "Then he'll grab and pinch. When he does, it's a sign he's ready to go back to his assisted living home."

"I'll keep it in mind," Sara said.

"So," Millie said in an obvious prelude to a change of subject, "are you packed and ready to go tomorrow?"

Sara smiled. "Almost. I just have to throw a few last-minute things into my bag and I'm ready. Cole, on the other hand, hasn't started. I'm going to work on his suitcase as soon as I get home."

Millie grinned. "Don't forget to pack a swim-suit. And that teddy we bought a few weeks ago."

"Those were the first things in the case," Sara answered, already looking forward to modeling the lacy negligee under her husband's admiring gaze. While most people thought they were going to enjoy ski slopes and mountain hikes, Sara had planned a far more private itinerary—an itiner-ary that focused only on the two of them.

"When are you leaving?" Millie asked.

"Our flight leaves early tomorrow morning. We'd thought about staying the night at one of the airport hotels, but it depends on Cole. You know how he is." Sara added, "He can't leave if he doesn't have every *i* dotted when it comes to his patients." She was convinced that was why everyone thought so highly of her husband—he didn't cut corners for convenience's sake.

She sighed. "Sometimes, his attention to detail is rather frustrating, especially when it interferes with our plans."

"Yeah, but you love him anyway."

Sara had half fallen in love with him the first day she'd met him, when he'd waltzed onto her floor as a first-year family medicine resident. She'd been suffering her own new-job jitters and he'd taken pity on her when she'd knocked a suture tray off the counter in obvious nervousness. The cup of coffee he'd subsequently bought her and the pep talk he'd delivered had marked the beginning of their professional and personal relationship.

"Yeah, I do," she said, returning Millie's grin with one of her own. "The only problem I have right now is knowing what to get him for Christmas. It's still two months away, but it'll be here before we know it."

"Has he mentioned anything that he wants?"

"Lots of things, but afterward he goes out and buys them for himself. I've told him not to do that, but so far it hasn't made an impression."

"It will when he wakes up on Christmas morning and there's nothing to open under the tree," Millie predicted. "Or you could just fill a box with socks and underwear."

"I could," Sara agreed, "but I couldn't be that cruel. I'm sure I'll get an idea this weekend."

"Well, good luck. As my mother always says, what do you get a man who has everything?"

What indeed? Sara thought. The one thing she'd wanted to give him—news that he'd be a father—wasn't something she could accomplish on her own, no matter how hard she wished for her dream to come true. Having grown up with a sister and two brothers, she wanted her house to ring with the same pitter-patter of footsteps as her parents' house had.

Be patient, Cole had reminded her. She'd try, she told herself. So what if it took them a little longer for their family to grow than she'd like? As long as it happened, as long as they loved each other, it would be worth the wait.

Fortunately, for the rest of her shift, she had little time to dwell on her personal plans, but the minute she left the hospital shortly after six o'clock, her thoughts raced ahead to her upcoming weekend.

Her excitement only grew when she found the lights blazing in their home and Cole's SUV parked in the garage. Pleased that Cole had finished earlier than she'd expected, she dashed through the cold garage and into her cozy house.

"This is a pleasant surprise," she called out to Cole from the mud room as she tugged off her gloves and hung her parka on a coat hook. "I honestly didn't think you'd make it home before eight."

He rose from his place at the table as she entered the kitchen and kissed her on the cheek. "Things turned out differently than we'd both anticipated," he answered with a tight smile that, with his strained expression, set off her mental radar. "How about some coffee?"

He turned away to dump several sweetener packets into his own mug. "You never drink caffeine at this time of night," she said as she watched his movements with a knot forming in her stomach. "What's wrong?"

"It's cold outside. How about hot tea instead?"

He was trying to distract her, which only meant that something was wrong. *Horribly* wrong. The knot tightened.

"Cole," she warned. "I know it's cold, but I'm not thirsty or hungry. Something is obviously on your mind. What is it?" As a thought occurred to her, she gasped. "Oh, no. We can't go on our trip, can we? Something happened and Chris can't cover for you at the hospital. Oh, Cole," she finished on a wail. "Not *again!*"

"Sara," he interrupted. "Stop jumping to conclusions. This isn't about my schedule. Just. Sit. Down."

She sat. With her hands clasped together in her lap, she waited. He sank onto the chair beside hers and carefully set his mug on the table. "An attorney spoke with me today."

Dread skittered down her spine. A lawyer never visited a physician with good news. "Is someone suing the hospital? And you?"

"No, nothing like that. Mr. Maitland is a partner in a law firm based in Tulsa."

"Tulsa?" Knowing he'd grown up in that area of Oklahoma, she asked, "Does this involve your relatives?"

"No."

"Then what did he want with you?"

"Do you remember reading the newspaper article about the medical helicopter crash the other day?"

"Yes. We'd talked about one of the nurses. I can't remember her name…"

"Ruth Warren," he supplied.

"Yeah. What about the crash?"

"As it turns out, I *did* know this particular Ruth Warren. Quite well, in fact."

His shock was understandable. She reached out to grab his hand, somewhat surprised by his cold fingers. "I'm sorry."

"In high school, we were good friends, although

I've only seen her once since then. At our class reunion a few years ago."

She furrowed her brow in thought. "You never mentioned a class reunion. When was this?"

"Remember those ten days in July, after you and I had broken up?"

"Yes," she said cautiously.

"During that time, I went to my class reunion. It was over the Fourth of July weekend, and I didn't have anything else to do, so I went."

"Really? Knowing how you've avoided going back to the area so you can't accidentally run into your relatives, I'm surprised."

"Yeah, well, it was a spur-of-the-moment decision," he said wryly. "Anyway, during that weekend, I met up with Ruth."

She touched his hand. "I'm glad you had a chance to reconnect with her after high school. Had you heard from her since then?"

"No. Not a word."

Sara had assumed as much because Cole had never mentioned her, but he was a closemouthed individual and often didn't mention those things he considered insignificant.

"Then what did the lawyer want?"

"He represents Ruth's estate. She named me, *us,* in her will."

Sara sat back in her chair, surprised. "She did? What did she do? Leave you her box of high school memorabilia?"

She'd expected her joke to make him smile, but it fell flat, which struck her as odd.

"She left us something more valuable than a box of dried corsages and school programs," he said evenly. "She entrusted the most important thing she had to us. Her son."

"Her son?" Of all the things he might have said, nothing was as shocking as this. "How old is he?"

"He's two and a half. His birthday was in April. April 2."

Surprise and shock gave way to excitement. "Oh, Cole," she said, reaching across the table to once again take his hand, her heart twisting at the thought of that motherless little boy. "He's practically a baby."

As she pondered the situation, she began to wonder why this woman had chosen them out of all the people she possibly could have known.

"Exactly why *did* she appoint us as his guardians? She never met me and you said yourself that you hadn't kept in contact with her. What about the boy's dad? Or her family? Didn't she have friends who were closer to her than you are? I'm not complaining, mind you. I'm only trying to understand why she gave him to people who are, for all intents and purposes, relative strangers, instead of choosing substitute parents who were within her current circle of friends."

"She had no family to speak of," he told her. "Ruth grew up in foster care and as soon as she graduated, she was on her own."

"If you hadn't seen her for three years, it's especially odd she'd ask us to take care of him. There has to be a connection—"

"There is," he said, clutching his mug with both hands. "But to explain it, I have something to confess."

Once again, warning bells clanged. "Okay," she said slowly.

"Ruth and I—that weekend we were together at the reunion…" he drew a deep breath as if bracing himself "…I did a stupid thing. Several stupid things, in fact. I was angry that you weren't satisfied with our relationship as it was—"

"Just living together," she interjected for clarification.

He nodded. "I was hurt that after all those years

of being a couple, you wouldn't be satisfied or happy until I put a ring on your finger."

"Oh, Cole," she said, disappointed that he hadn't fully understood why she'd pressed him to take their relationship to the next level. "It wasn't about flashing a gold band or a huge diamond. It was what the ring *represented*—a commitment to spend the rest of our lives together."

"I realized that. Later. But during that first week we were apart, while I was angry and hurt and feeling everything in between, I went to my reunion and…" he took another deep breath "…drank a few too many margaritas. A *lot* too many." He paused.

She was surprised to learn that Cole—a man who couldn't even be classified as a moderate drinker—had over-imbibed. While she wasn't condoning his action, she figured most people had done so at one time or another. His actions weren't smart or ideal, but drinking too much on one occasion wasn't an unforgivable offense, in her opinion, even if at the time he'd been old enough to know better.

"And?" she coaxed.

"When I saw Ruth again—we confided a lot in each other during our teen years—we talked.

We both unloaded on each other and she helped me admit a few hard truths—"

"Do you mean to say that your friend *Ruth* convinced you to propose?" She'd always believed that he'd come to that conclusion on his own. It was disappointing to imagine that he'd been persuaded to marry her not because he loved her but because of a relative stranger's advice.

"Ruth didn't convince me to do anything," he insisted. "She pointed out what I already knew but couldn't quite admit—that I loved you and couldn't imagine my life without you—which was why I was so angry and hurt and miserable. And if I loved you, then I had to face my fears and propose."

Fears? He'd been *afraid?*

"Wait a minute." She held up her hands to forestall him so she could sort through his confession. "You'd always said that you wouldn't marry until you were ready, but now I learn that you were *scared?* Why didn't you explain? We could have discussed this."

"If you'll recall, we'd tried, but the conversation deteriorated and you walked out."

She wanted to protest that he could have stopped her, or that he could have called, or he

could have done any number of things, but placing blame at this date was silly.

"Okay," she said evenly, "both of us could have
done things differently, but truly, Cole, what were
you afraid of?"

"That I couldn't be the husband you wanted or
needed. That our relationship would change. We
were doing great just living together and I had
this…this *fear*…that marriage might ruin what
we had."

"How was that possible?" she asked, incredulous. "We'd been living together for two years
and dated for a year prior to that. How did you
think marriage would ruin—?"

"You forget that the last functional family relationship I was in ended when I was eight. What
did *I* know about how a healthy marriage should
be? By the time I started college, I didn't know if
the happy home I remembered was real or make-
believe. Do you really wonder why I might be
afraid our relationship would change, and not for
the better? And when it did, both of us would be
stuck in an untenable situation."

She fell silent as she processed the information.
"Okay, I can respect that, but you obviously faced
your fears because you found me at my friend's

house and proposed." It bothered her to think that he could discuss his fears with a woman he hadn't seen in years instead of with her, but there was little she could do about it now. She only hoped he wouldn't tell her that at the time asking her to marry him had simply been the lesser of two evils.

"Proposing—marrying you—was the best decision I ever made. Don't ever forget that."

His vehemence both surprised and alarmed her. "Okay," she said warily. "But meanwhile you had your heart-to-heart with Ruth and because you two drowned your sorrows together, she wanted you to raise her child if something happened to her."

He visibly winced and avoided her gaze. "Unfortunately, we did more than talk and drown our sorrows."

The bottom dropped out of her stomach. "Oh, Cole. Please don't tell me that you— That you and this high school friend…"

He nodded, his expression grave. "We slept together. We didn't plan it, I swear. I didn't even know she was going to *be* at the reunion. The combination of everything from my insecurities and alcohol level to Ruth needing her own listening ear all coalesced until events just…happened. I've never done anything like that before or since and I regretted it right away. You have to believe me."

A part of her brain heard his near-desperation, but she was still too numbed by his newest revelation to grant him absolution.

"You should have told me," she said as her whole body seemed to turn into ice. "We should have had this conversation as soon as you rolled back into town. About your doubts and your… and Ruth."

"I couldn't," he admitted. "I was too embarrassed and ashamed. I didn't go to my reunion intending to do anything but meet with old friends. After my lapse in judgment—" his voice was rueful "—I knew this news would be devastating and even though we technically weren't a couple at the time it happened, I couldn't risk my mistake potentially destroying our future."

Would she have refused to marry him if she'd known he'd slept with another woman? Knowing how devastated she'd been at the time he'd stormed out after their argument, hearing that would have probably convinced her to count her blessings that he'd walked away.

At this point, however, she didn't know for certain what she might have done. She might only have extended their engagement until she'd been fully persuaded that he hadn't entertained second thoughts about marriage, but one truth remained undeniable. He'd taken away her opportunity to choose.

"I can't begin to tell you how sorry I am," he added. "If I could turn back the clock and live that night over, I would."

His remorse seemed genuine, but it did little to ease her sense of betrayal. "Sorry that it happened or sorry that you told me?"

He didn't have to explain, her little voice pointed out. *He could have simply let the story stand that they were old friends who'd reconnected during a class reunion. You'd still never know...*

"There isn't a day that goes by that I don't feel regret for my actions," he said, meeting her gaze. "That's something I have to live with for the rest of my life."

The pain in his eyes wasn't feigned; she recognized that. Unfortunately, his revelation made her question so many things. Had he *really* wanted to marry her, or had he only asked her because he'd found his courage in the bottom of a bottle?

How many other secrets had he kept from her? He probably had many, because there were so many personal topics he refused to discuss.

And yet, technically, they *had* severed their relationship, which meant he hadn't been required to answer to her. No vows had been broken at the time he and Ruth…

But it still hurt to know that he'd fallen into bed with another woman so quickly. Granted, the alcohol and his own anger had contributed to his decision, but still…

Although the truth weighed heavily, she had to give credit where it was due. He'd been a faithful husband for the past three years and he'd been honest when he could have kept this secret forever and no one would have ever known. Yet he'd taken the risk and apologized profusely rather than simply brush off the incident.

Emotionally, she wanted to bristle and remain angry, but logically the incident was over and done with. Walking away from him because of one relatively *ancient* mistake committed when they'd been separated suggested her love must be terribly shallow if she couldn't forgive and forget.

"Sara?" he asked tentatively.

She exhaled a long, drawn-out sigh and offered a tremulous smile. "As disappointed as I am, as betrayed as I feel, even though some would say I shouldn't, I can't change the past. We'll leave it there, shall we?"

"Unfortunately, there's more," he said.

"More?" she asked, incredulous. "What more can there be? Isn't this *friendship* you had—" she chose that word instead of "affair" because she didn't know if a one-night stand fit the true definition "—the reason why she wanted you to look after her child?"

He didn't answer at first. "Sara," he said softly, "Brody is thirty months old. His second birthday came during the first part of April."

"Yes, you already told me."

He rubbed the back of his neck. "Do the math."

She did. Then, with a sinking heart, she knew. The apology on his face confirmed it.

"Oh. My. God. He's your son, too."

If Sara's face had revealed her shock before, now Cole only saw horror. From her sudden intake of breath, the oxygen in the room had vanished with the news, just as it had when Parker Maitland had delivered the same bombshell to him a few hours ago. This news had knocked his world off its axis, just as it had for his wife.

Eternity had only lasted forty-eight hours.

An unholy dread had filled him from that moment on because he would have to explain the inexplicable to Sara. His confession had crushed her, just as he'd suspected it would, and, just as he'd feared, the light in her eyes had faded. Already she stared at him as if he'd become someone she didn't know.

How ironic to be in this position. After spending his entire life always weighing his options and plotting his course carefully to avoid potential pitfalls, *the one time* he'd acted impulsively would haunt him for ever.

Oh, he could have ended this earlier without Sara ever being the wiser. He could have told the lawyer that he didn't want to raise Ruth's son—and his—and all this would have vanished like morning mist on a hot summer day. Yet he couldn't build one lie upon another, no matter how enticing the idea was. Untruths always had a tendency to be revealed.

"You had a baby with this Ruth person."

She sounded dazed, much as he had when he'd heard the news. "Apparently so."

"Are you certain? I mean, if she slept with you at your reunion, she might have spent time with someone else, too."

Her faith in him was bittersweet and only made him feel worse than he already did. He, too, had posed the question, hoping there'd been some misunderstanding, but the possibility had died an instant death after Maitland had presented him with undeniable proof.

"She didn't," he assured her, hating to destroy her hopes but understanding how the possibility was a lifeline for her to grab—a lifeline that their life wouldn't be turned upside down so easily. "Maitland gave me a picture of the boy. There's a strong…family resemblance."

It was more than a resemblance. The phrase "chip off the old block" came to mind. If he compared photos of himself at that age, he'd think his image had been cut and pasted into a scene from today.

"And she wants you to look after her—your—child."

From past experience, Cole knew that Sara's

reserved tone was merely a smoke screen, especially given the words she'd chosen. *Her. Your child.* Underneath her deadly calm was a churning cauldron of emotions held in check by sheer force of will. Cole would have rather seen her yell, scream or throw things, instead of seeing her so controlled.

"She wants *us* to look after him," he corrected. "She wanted Brody to have two parents, not one."

As she sat frozen, Cole hastened to continue. "Apparently, Ruth knew the situation would be… difficult…which was why she left a letter for you to read."

He dug in the manila envelope Maitland had given him and placed the small sealed white envelope that bore Sara's name in front of her. Next to it, he positioned Brody's photograph so that those impish dark brown eyes were facing her.

Sara didn't move to accept the envelope or glance at the picture.

"Ruth rightly believed you would play an important role in Brody's upbringing, which is why she stipulated that you also had to agree to take him."

"And if I don't?"

He paused, torn between wanting her to refuse

and hoping she'd accept the challenge ahead of them. "Then the search will begin for different parents," he said evenly. "According to Maitland, Ruth hoped that wouldn't happen. He and his wife, Eloise, were Ruth's neighbors and they knew how much she worried about Brody going into the same foster-care system she had."

"If they knew Ruth so well, why didn't she appoint them as his substitute parents?"

"Parker is sixty-nine and Eloise is sixty-seven. As much as they love Brody, it isn't feasible for them to parent a child at their age." Parker had told him that he and Ruth had discussed this scenario and they'd both agreed that Brody needed younger parents who would conceivably give him siblings as well as live long enough to see him through high school and college.

"Where is he now?"

"He's with Maitland and his wife at a hotel." He paused. "Parker invited us to stop by at our convenience tonight. However, he did mention that Brody usually goes to bed at eight and with all the commotion of the past few days, he's been a little cranky if he stays up later than that."

The silence in the room became deafening and Cole watched helplessly as Sara rubbed her forehead with a shaky hand. "I don't know what to say," she murmured. "I'm tempted to believe I'm dreaming, that this is just an elaborate hoax or a misunderstanding."

"I know how you feel, but this…" he fingered the photo "…proves otherwise."

He stared at the snapshot lying on the table, picking out the facial features that seemed to be carbon copies of his own—coal-black hair, dimples, a straight nose and lopsided grin. Yet, even with the proof before him, he was still hardly able to accept that he had a son.

A *son.*

While he'd been willing to add to their family—*someday* in the future—knowing he had a son *now* was mind-boggling. It was one thing to feel guilty about his one-night stand, but quite another to know a child had resulted. He didn't know if he felt happy or sad, disappointed or excited, but he'd sort through those emotions later. At this moment, the reality had to be addressed, which was, namely, would they accept Brody into their home, or would Brody enter the same state-run children's services that Ruth had loathed?

He simply couldn't go against Ruth's wishes, but her way was filled with pitfalls. Having grown up in a situation where he hadn't been wanted, he'd always vowed to keep some sort of "escape clause" in his relationships, which was why he'd had so much trouble making a commitment to Sara. But now, if he accepted Ruth's child, *his* son, there would be no escape. If he intended to do this, he had to do so with the intent of being in it for the long haul.

This, at least, was the same decision he'd made before he'd proposed. And that had worked out, hadn't it? he told himself.

Or, it had, until he'd lost all common sense on that long-ago night.

He wanted to scream at the fates for putting him in this position, but what was done was done. There was only one way to escape this time, but as he glanced at Brody's photo, the idea didn't appeal as much as it might have. After all, if he'd been willing to face his fears and have a baby with Sara, how was this any different?

There was a big difference, he thought tiredly. Sara was his wife and she'd stand beside him, helping him, guiding him along the right path, correcting his mistakes. Now the question was, would she stay with him or not? Would he lose his son *and* his wife?

He studied her, wishing she'd say or do something rather than remain locked in icy calm. If only they had time to come to terms with the situation and what it meant to them as a couple, but time was a luxury they didn't have.

"Sara?" he asked tentatively. "We have to make a decision."

"Right *now?*" She sounded horrified.

"Maybe not this instant," he conceded, "but definitely within the next twenty-four hours. Brody's future has to be settled, one way or another. Keeping him in limbo isn't in his best interests."

He'd wondered if the prospect of having the baby she'd wanted would overshadow its origins, but she clearly hadn't reached that level of acceptance yet. He understood. He was still stunned and he'd felt the bombshell several hours earlier.

She nodded, almost absentmindedly.

Thinking that Sara would benefit from seeing Ruth's wishes in black and white, he pulled a copy of the will out of the manila envelope and flipped to the pages in question.

"Ruth had arranged for all of her assets to be placed into a trust fund for Brody and she named us as the trustees. She didn't want finances to factor in to our decision, so she left a modest nest egg for his care."

Not that he intended to tap into it if they chose to raise him. After all, Brody was *his* son, and his responsibility.

"There are a few personal things she asked that we keep for him, heirlooms if you will. Everything else will be sold."

"I see."

"She also asked that we legally adopt him so he carries our surname rather than hers."

"She thought of everything, didn't she?" she said wryly.

"I'm sure she and her legal counsel tried to cover every contingency."

"Did she have a plan if we decided not to raise her child?"

Cole's cautious optimism fell as Sara asked this same question for a second time, as if she wanted to be sure she had other options.

"As I said earlier, Ruth had hoped you wouldn't make that choice."

"Did she make a plan B?" Sara pressed on, as if through gritted teeth.

Cole sighed. "She did. Brody will become a

ward of the state and will be eligible for adoption by another couple."

In that instant, he knew he was facing an untenable situation. Ruth had guessed correctly that he wouldn't be able to easily give up his son, but if Sara wasn't in favor of keeping him, he'd be forced to choose between his wife and a boy he'd just learned was his. Neither was a palatable option.

Still, he wanted to think positive...

She frowned. "Wouldn't you have to relinquish your rights if you're his father?"

He'd wondered if she would have realized that. While everything within him fought that idea, the letter Ruth had left for his eyes only had requested him to do just that if Sara wouldn't agree to her terms.

I know how difficult this would be for you, Ruth had written, *but you know far better than I how much harder Brody's life would be to live in a home where one parental figure didn't want him...*

He might not want to sign those documents, and his decision would haunt him if he did, but he'd do it, for Brody's sake. "Yes," he said simply, hating the mere notion of it. "I would."

And he'd regret it for the rest of his life.

She paused. The wrinkle between her eyebrows suggested she was weighing her options. "And if we take him?" she finally asked. "What then?"

A spark of optimism flared. "Then, starting tomorrow, he'll spend time with us. The Maitlands will stay in town for a few days to ease his transition but they can't stay longer because they have family commitments of their own."

"That's it? He just moves in?"

"More or less. There are several legal details to take care of during the next few days and weeks but, to be honest, I can't remember what Maitland told me they were. As soon as we come to an agreement, they'll arrange for the personal belongings to be shipped here."

"But all of this hinges on our decision."

As far as he was concerned, there wasn't a decision to make. The thought of committing himself to the responsibility of another human being who would depend upon him for years to come might send a cold shiver down his spine—a fact that Ruth had known full well—but he couldn't deny her request, not just because Brody was his own son but because it was time to face his fears.

Unfortunately, the decision wasn't completely his to make.

It was ironic to think that Sara would have jumped for joy at taking in Brody had someone else fathered him. Unfortunately, Brody's presence would not only be a visual and constant reminder of his error in judgment but also that she'd lost her own child. The only question was, could she look past those reminders or not?

"Yes," he answered simply, threading his fingers together in a white-knuckled grip. "Keep in mind he has nowhere else to go."

She met his gaze. "That's not fair, Cole. Don't play on my sympathies to get what you obviously want."

"I'm only stating a fact."

Slowly, she rose, leaving the photo on the table. "I won't apologize for needing time."

"Okay," he conceded, "but—"

She held up her hands. "I can't rush into a decision without thinking this through. The thing is, whatever we—I—decide to do about your son, our lives will never be the same."

As if he needed to be reminded… He was damned if he did, and damned if he didn't. Sara must have come to the same realization, too.

Suddenly, holding a person's life in his hands, medically speaking, seemed like less of a mine-field than the situation looming ahead of him. Although he'd mentioned a twenty-four-hour deadline, somehow he sensed that announcing the Maitlands were expecting a decision by to-morrow morning wouldn't be well received.

He watched helplessly as she walked out of the room.

As he sat alone, he thought about how he'd enjoyed almost three years of blissful ignorance. Ruth should have told him and the fact she hadn't angered him. He had deserved to know, damn it!

Like Sara deserved to know? his little voice asked. *You wanted to protect your relationship with Sara, so maybe Ruth was doing the same for you...*

He sighed as he recognized the truth. Ruth's silence *had* provided a simpler solution to their dilemma. She'd known how crazily in love he'd been with Sara and breaking the news would have driven a wedge into his new marriage. Not only that, Ruth would have had to share Brody with him because as unprepared as he felt about fatherhood, he would have insisted on knowing his own son, even if he'd been a long-distance parent.

The idea that he might never have known about Brody if Ruth hadn't died didn't set well and was too close to his own situation for comfort. His only aunt and uncle hadn't bothered to make contact with him until he was eight, when circumstances had forced them to do so. While Brody's fate was still undecided, he certainly wouldn't ignore the boy in the meantime.

Idly, he wondered if this one subtle difference proved that his fears of repeating his relatives' dysfunctional behavior were unfounded. Of course, wanting to meet Brody was hardly enough evidence to make a case, but it was a difference that he could think about and consider. In the meantime, he had more pressing concerns...

The clock on the microwave showed six-thirty. Had only thirty minutes passed since he'd broken the news to Sara? Thirty minutes since he'd shattered his wife's faith in him?

He glanced at the sealed envelope on the table before focusing on the photo of his son. *His son.* A living, breathing product of his own DNA, a continuation of the Wittman family tree.

The same awed thoughts had bombarded him

after Sara had announced her pregnancy but this time the feelings were a little different. Now he had a name and face whereas before the only tangible evidence of his child had been a number on her lab report. Before he'd had time to dream big dreams, to imagine a little boy or girl with Sara's beautiful eyes and his crooked smile, or to work through his reservations about being a parent, Sara had miscarried.

Brody, however, was here. In the flesh. Already walking and talking with a personality of his own.

Suddenly, the past two-plus years of ignorant bliss were far too long. He wanted to meet his son *tonight,* regardless of the hour or how cranky he might be. Waiting until tomorrow seemed like an eternity.

As he heard a loud thump coming from the direction of their bedroom, however, his eagerness faded. Meeting a child he might never be able to claim as his own could easily be a prelude to heartache.

CHAPTER TWO

SARA stared at the suitcase she'd dumped unceremoniously on the floor and sat on the edge of the bed. Whether she unpacked or not, their trip was over. Done. Finished. If they took in Brody, they wouldn't go. And if they didn't, they still wouldn't go because these events had killed her romantic-weekend mood.

Oh, who was she kidding? Tonight's revelation had ruined more than the weekend. It had completely cracked the foundation of their marriage. Complete collapse was only a nudge away.

The question was, did she want to give their marriage that nudge, or not? Half of her was tempted beyond belief. The other half encouraged her to weather the storm.

She had to think. She had to decide what was the best option, which was the better course, but her emotions were far too raw to make a logical decision. Leaving meant the end of every hope and dream she'd nurtured.

Staying meant…meant what? That she'd already forgiven Cole? She hadn't. That she loved him? At the moment, it was questionable.

Whatever her choice, she had to make it for the right reasons. Right now, she felt as if she were balanced precariously on a wet log, struggling to maintain her footing while knowing it wouldn't take much for her to fall in either direction. With a decision this monumental looming over her, she needed time.

Not making a decision was making a decision.

Not true, she argued with herself. She wasn't choosing to stay or go. She was simply choosing to give herself time to come to terms with the fact that Cole had a son.

He had a son.

Without her.

Once again, much as it had when she'd first connected the dots, hurt and anger crashed over her in debilitating waves. She kicked the luggage defiantly, well aware it was a poor substitute for the man who deserved her wrath, but she still hoped that small act would ease her pain.

It didn't.

She hoisted the case back on the bed and unzipped the top. In spite of her rough treatment, the clothes inside were just as neat as when she'd placed them there. Once again, she was racked with indecision.

"Are you okay, Sara?" Cole asked from the doorway, a worried wrinkle on his forehead.

"I'm just peachy," she answered waspishly. "How do you *think* I am?"

He didn't answer, as if he knew the answer. "May I come in?"

"Suit yourself." She spied the edge of the black silk teddy she'd purchased specifically for this weekend and poked it underneath her jeans and sweatshirts to keep it out of sight.

"Are you unpacking?" he asked.

"Yes." She eyed the case and suddenly didn't feel inclined to empty it, especially when the urge to grab it and run away was far too strong. "No. I'm not sure."

"Maybe this will help. Packing means you're leaving. To stay, you have to *un*pack."

He sounded calm, as if he were simply helping her decide between wearing a pair of blue or green scrubs. "I realize that," she answered sharply. Then, realizing she sounded shrewish, she softened her tone. "I'm trying to decide. Unfortunately, I can't decide what is the right thing to do." She rubbed at the crease on her forehead.

"I know you're upset," he began as he crossed the threshold.

"Wow. Whatever gave you that idea? Why would I possibly be upset to hear that my husband…" Her voice cracked. "My husband had a child with another woman while we were separated? My God, Cole. It was only a week. *One lousy week.*"

"Actually, it was ten days," he corrected, "but, yes, those were lousy days on so many levels."

She brushed aside his comment. "One week, ten days, it's practically the same thing. All I know is that I didn't fall into bed with anyone during that time, even if I *technically…*" she made imaginary quotation marks in the air "…could have."

"It was a one-night error in judgment. It didn't mean a thing."

"Oh, that's wonderful, Cole. I'm sure Brody will be happy to hear his dad say that he was a mistake. An error in judgment."

"I only meant—"

"The point is," she continued, "I haven't forgotten why we split up or why we got back together."

"I haven't either," he said evenly.

She rubbed the back of her neck. "But now you're asking me to ignore what you did and welcome your son with open arms."

His expression grew grave. "I'm only trying to explain what happened. While I know it's too soon to ask for forgiveness, I'd like you to understand—"

"I'm having trouble with that," she said flatly. "The Cole Wittman I knew prided himself on his control and for you to do something so obviously *out* of control...well, it makes me look at our life together in a different light, which is why I can't decide...about this." She motioned toward her suitcase.

"I knew the situation would be...tough to handle," he admitted. "If it's any consolation, I've dreaded telling you from the moment Maitland showed me Ruth's will. I expected the news would be hard for you to swallow."

At least he was cognizant enough of her feelings to guess at her reaction. "You were right."

"I'm sorry to have landed us in this predicament."

Predicament was such an insipid term for the situation they were in, she decided.

"Would you rather I'd kept this from you and told Maitland then and there that we weren't interested in taking Brody?"

It would have been so much easier, she thought with irritation, but she also knew that "easy" didn't always mean "better." Successful marriages were built on honesty, not secrets, and if Cole had kept this from her—even if part of her wished he had—they could be setting a dangerous precedent for their future relationship. What would stop him from withholding information from her again, especially if he deemed it was information she'd find uncomfortable?

"Why didn't you?" she asked, curious.

He shrugged. "The truth eventually comes out. Maybe not today or next month or next year, but sometime down the road it would surface again. Fate has a way of doing the unexpected," he said wryly, "and I figured that learning about Brody would be easier to handle now rather than in ten or twenty years.

"And," he continued tentatively, "knowing how badly you wanted a baby, I'd hoped…" His voice faded.

"That I'd overlook Brody's origins because he would satisfy my own need?" she asked icily.

He had the grace to wince. "Something like that."

"You were wrong. Yes, I want us to have a baby, but only because a child is a logical extension of our love for each other. While I'd be happy to adopt a child, too, the fact that Brody is yours and not a stranger's makes this situation unique. There's another layer of emotional baggage that has to be dealt with."

He nodded, his face lined with a combination of resignation and misery. "I know."

"You're placing me in a no-win situation," she pointed out. "You realize that, don't you?"

"It isn't a no-win," he insisted. "If we can't agree on Brody's future, then that's the end of it."

His even tone wasn't reassuring because in her gut she knew this wouldn't be the end. For the rest of their lives together, if she denied Ruth's request, the what-ifs would plague them.

On the other hand, if she walked away from Cole and the situation, she'd lose as much if not more.

"You want to bring him home, don't you?" That

observation was irritating in itself. While she'd been eager to start the process of fertility testing, Cole had been content to bide their time, claiming he was happy with or without a baby. Now, though, he was almost falling over his own feet to welcome his secret child into their household.

In a distant corner of her heart she knew she was being unfair, but at this moment she was still too crushed by a multitude of emotions to be rational.

"I do, but not if we aren't in agreement. We're a team, Sara. We have to function like one. Besides, you're the one with the strong family background. Without your support, I can't be his father, or anyone else's," he said flatly.

The idea that he needed *her* to do this job mollified her to some degree. It also helped to hear that her husband—a brilliant, meticulous, caring physician who'd graduated in the top ten percent of his medical school class—suffered from a few feelings of inadequacy, too. Unfortunately, could she trust him again? She didn't realize she'd voiced her thought until he answered.

"We've had nearly three wonderful years together," he said simply. "And three before that.

Have I given you any reason to doubt me during the time we've been together?"

"I presume 'together' is the operative word?"

Her barb had struck home because he fell silent. "I deserve that, I suppose, but I'm the same man I was yesterday, the day before, last week and last year. I love you more now than ever and I don't ever want to hurt you. Every decision I make is tested against that standard. Yes, on that one occasion, I let my fear overrule my good sense. Yes, I drank more than I should have and, yes, I made a bad choice that I'll regret for the rest of my days, but I don't want to lose you over this, Sara. I…I *can't*."

The solution to this utterly devastating change in their circumstances was simple. Leave the past in the past and focus on the future. Unfortunately, that was easier said than done, especially when she would face the proof of his poor choice every day for the rest of her life.

Could she do it? Could she ignore how his son had been conceived? Could she let go of her anger and her sense of betrayal even if Cole had been a free agent at the time?

She had to, otherwise she might as well walk out now with her packed suitcase. As her mother had always cautioned her, "Don't do anything in the heat of the moment. You'll always live with your regrets." At this moment, her emotions were too raw to think rationally, so she cautioned herself to bide her time until she could approach the situation sensibly.

On the other hand, the difficulty she had went much deeper than the notion of having Cole's child underfoot. It was the reminder that Ruth had succeeded in one night with what she had failed to achieve for months. If that wasn't enough to howl at life's unfairness, she didn't know what would be.

"I'd do anything if I could turn back the clock," he said quietly, "but I can't."

He sounded sincere. She wanted to believe that he'd never done anything like this before or since, and part of her *did* believe, but her heart was still too bruised to forgive. Given enough time, she hoped she would, but at this moment she couldn't.

"I know you want me to smile and say everything's okay. That I'll unpack so we can bring Brody home and be one big happy family, but I can't say those things." She met his gaze. "I *can't*. Not yet."

He fell silent. "I can respect that, but while

you're mulling over the situation, we need to meet him, Sara. I *need* to see him. Not just a photo, but *him*. Brody didn't arrive under ideal conditions, but he's my son."

She'd half anticipated his request. What man wouldn't be curious about his own flesh and blood? She, on the other hand, wasn't eager to meet the little person that he and another woman had produced so easily.

"If you're asking for permission, feel free to do whatever you want."

"I'd like you to go with me," he said.

She shook her head. "I can't. Not yet. Not tonight."

Expecting him to protest, she was surprised when he simply paused. "Okay," he said, weariness evident in those two syllables. "If you can't handle seeing him so soon, you can't. I'll call Maitland and decline his invitation."

As he rose and strolled toward the door, his usually squared shoulders slumped in defeat, she regretted being so petty. The thing was, she already guessed at how this situation would play out and she was simply trying to hold it at bay as long as she could, hoping another solution would present itself or, better yet, she'd wake up soon and discover this was only a nightmare.

As Cole had said, the boy's future had to be decided. How could she possibly make the right choice if she didn't face her demons? He was, after all, Cole's son no matter how, why or when he had been conceived. Being with Brody would be a painful experience whether she met him tonight, tomorrow or next week, so she had to handle it like one handled any adhesive bandage. Rip off the tape in one swift motion rather than by degrees. Besides, she'd always faced her problems head-on. Ignoring them, pretending they didn't exist, wasn't her way, even if she wanted to indulge herself.

"Cole, wait," she said as he reached the threshold.

He stopped and turned. "Yeah?"

"Would you really cancel and stay home tonight?"

"If that's what you wanted," he said simply. "I may not be the most sensitive fellow in the world, but I'm well aware that seeing the boy won't be easy for you. If giving you more time to adjust will help, then that's what we'll do."

It would have been so much easier if he'd been

less thoughtful, less understanding, but he was being all those things and more, which meant she had to respond in kind.

"Unfortunately, I'm not sure there's enough time in the world to do that," she said wryly. "So…" she drew a shaky breath "…we should put this first meeting behind us."

His gaze narrowed. "Are you sure?"

"No." Her smile wobbled. "But it won't be any easier tomorrow."

"Probably not.

"But after we visit, what happens if I decide I can't be his mother?" *Or your wife?* she mentally added.

He hesitated, his expression uncertain. "Let's take this one step at a time, shall we? When we come home, we'll talk. All I ask is for you to consider the possibilities."

She only hoped she could.

Sara walked with Cole toward the Maitlands' hotel room, lost in her thoughts. Cole had explained and apologized both profusely and sincerely, but until she came to terms with what had happened, talking about those long-ago events seemed futile. She'd never imagined their future would become as muddled as it was at this moment, but muddled it was. Now she steeled herself for what would come next.

"Come in, come in," a tall, white-haired Parker Maitland welcomed them far more warmly than Sara felt inside. "Eloise and I were just reading Brody a bedtime story."

Without looking at Cole—she still found it difficult to meet his gaze because if she did, she'd break down and now wasn't the time to fall apart—she crossed the threshold.

Inside, she found Eloise, a petite woman with salt-and-pepper hair, sitting against the pillows with a small, dark-headed boy wearing racecar flannel pajamas plastered against her.

Eloise smiled at her as she continued reading from her book about the exploits of a puppy. While she read, Sara watched the youngster's bright eyes follow the pictures, indicating how intent he was on the story. When Eloise said clearly, "The end," the youngster smiled, giggled, then flipped the book to the beginning and said plainly, "Again!"

"Not again," Eloise said firmly. "We have guests who want to say hello to you."

Taking their presence in obvious stride, Brody

took the book, climbed off the bed and ran toward her. "Owie," he said, presenting his thumb to Sara.

She dutifully examined the nearly invisible scratch across the knuckle. "I see," she said as she crouched down for a better view. "Does it hurt?"

"Kiss?" he asked.

"Will that make your finger feel better?" she asked as the ice in her chest began to crack under his innocent friendliness.

He bobbed his head, so she kissed the spot, feeling his tiny bones in her hand as she smelled his bath-scented little-boy smell. His was a request guaranteed to enchant, and in spite of her reservations she was touched by his trust in an apparent stranger. It would have been so much easier if he'd run away from her and hid...but, no, he'd approached her with the assurance that, although she was a new face, she wouldn't reject him.

She wanted to, she really did. She wanted to walk out of the room and pretend the past few hours had never happened, but it was impossible. She held this child's future in her hands.

No, she held all three of their futures in her hands.

As sympathetic as she was to Brody's situation, she still had one question she couldn't answer. Was she strong enough to welcome Cole's son by another woman into her home when up until a few hours ago she'd always imagined it would be *her* son or daughter she carried across the threshold?

Happy with the attention his finger had received, Brody turned to Cole and presented him with his book. "Again," he repeated, this time with a lopsided grin resembling Cole's so closely that it was painful to see.

Master Brody was his father's son, from the cowlick in his dark hair to the cute dimple in his right cheek.

She'd secretly feared that once Cole met his son, he wouldn't be able to let him go. If the awe in his eyes, the benevolent smile on his face and the shaky hand as he gently stroked Brody's baby-fine hair were any indication, she was right.

Perhaps it might have been easier to watch the two together if she hadn't studied Brody closely enough to decide that his pointy chin and eyes were visible reminders of his mother.

Reminders that Cole had poured out his troubles to a woman he hadn't seen in years. Reminders that this same woman, after one night, had given Cole what she could not after all this time. Obviously, *she,* Sara Jean Wittman, was at fault for everything from her miscarriage to her failure to get pregnant.

She wanted to weep with frustration and disappointment and when she was finished, she wanted to hate the faceless Ruth for being so fertile while she was not. Shouldn't the love she felt for her husband carry some weight with cosmic fates? Obviously not.

As she watched Cole and Brody together, saw Brody's curiosity about this new man who was willing to read his story again, two choices lay before her in stark black and white.

She could be the bad guy and stop everything pertaining to Brody's guardianship, but if she did, Cole would never forgive her. Oh, he said he'd accept her decision, but that had been before he'd seen Brody and been exposed to his winsome ways. There would always be a hole inside him that she would never be able to fill.

On the other hand, could she be Brody's mother? Could she handle the constantly visible reminder of her failure to give him a child of *their* own—a child who represented *their* love and devotion? The little boy needed and deserved a mom who would nurture him as much as his had. Would she shortchange *him* if she wasn't completely sold on the idea?

Answers eluded her.

While Cole read the story one more time, Sara visited with the Maitlands, although admittedly she couldn't remember any part of their conversation afterward because she'd focused most of her attention on her husband and his son.

This time, when the end was declared and the book closed, Brody yawned and his eyelids drooped, but he simply snuggled against Cole as if he intended to fall asleep in his lap.

Sara was certain Cole would be more than happy to let him.

"We probably should go," Cole said, his tone wistful as he stared down at the little boy.

"We should," Sara agreed, more than ready for a chance to distance herself from the situation—and her impending decision. "Brody needs his rest."

"We're really glad you came by," Eloise told Sara with a smile. "I know you and your husband have a lot to discuss."

Sara glanced at Cole. His longing expression only sent her spirits into a deeper nosedive, but she pasted a smile on her face. "Yes, we do."

Her heart, however, insisted otherwise. They didn't have anything to discuss. Not one simple point had to be debated because in that instant she was reminded of her marriage vows... *For better, for worse...*

This definitely fell in the "for worse" category.

Regardless of how she classified their new circumstances, those vows made her path clear— the same path that was uneven and strewn with boulders of varying sizes, the same path that it would be easier *not* to travel on. In spite of her reluctance, in spite of her reservations, in spite of the small vindictive streak that demanded retribution, she couldn't deny Cole the opportunity to parent his own son. Neither could she deny Brody the opportunity to know his father.

Oh, she could, of course, but it would be the beginning of the end of their marriage and deep down she didn't believe she wanted that.

She simply *had* to welcome Brody into their home and learn how to deal with her jumbled emotions.

* * *

Normally, Sara snuggled against Cole when they climbed into bed but not tonight. For the first time ever, she remained on her side of the mattress, curled into a ball with her back toward him.

He sighed, wishing he knew the right words to break the silence as frigid as the great outdoors. He'd already apologized, but repeating himself wasn't breaking through the barrier between them.

He deserved her wrath, he supposed, but didn't six years of being together—minus one week— mean anything? He also knew he was asking a lot of her to raise his son when she so desperately wanted her own, but what else could he have done? Turning Brody over to someone else would rip open the scars on his heart that Sara hadn't realized she'd healed.

As the silence grew to unbearable proportions, he knew from her steady breathing and the occasional sniffly hiccup that she wasn't asleep. He wanted to reach out and draw her next to him in order to give as well as receive comfort but, given her mood, he might end up with a black eye. Still, the possibility was worth the risk.

He reached out and hauled her against him.

"What are you doing?" she asked, her body tense.

"Holding you."

"I don't want to be held," she said, although she didn't attempt to move away.

"Too bad."

"I'm not making love with you."

"I wasn't offering," he said with equanimity.

"In fact, if our second bedroom was furnished for guests, I'd be sleeping in there."

He didn't doubt it. From the moment he'd silently followed her into the house, he'd mentally prepared himself to watch her grab her still-packed suitcase and leave. As the evening had worn on and they'd gone through the motions of their normal routine of watching the ten o'clock news and weather broadcast before going to bed, he'd slowly grown more optimistic.

At the moment, though, he was grateful that the only other available room in their house was being used as their home office.

"So just because I'm sharing this bed with you doesn't mean you're off the proverbial hook," she added. "As far as I'm concerned, our relationship is on indefinite probation."

He had suspected as much when she hadn't unpacked her clothes. Instead, she'd simply set the case near the wall, ready to grab at a moment's notice.

All he could do was take heart that she wasn't calling it quits. Probation, not to mention the suitcase standing in their bedroom rather than at the front door, meant he still had a chance…

"Indefinite?" he asked. "Seems like a long time, but we can debate that topic another day."

"I assume you have a different subject in mind?" she asked coolly. "Your son, perhaps?"

She knew him too well, he thought ruefully. He hated to press her for a decision about Brody, but as he'd told her before they'd left the house, they'd talk after they met the boy. Ever since they'd left the hotel, she hadn't said more than a few words. Now was as good a time as any for conversation. "Yeah. We should discuss—"

"Was she pretty?"

In spite of the conversational detour, he instinctively knew she was asking about Ruth. He paused, trying to remember the woman who'd only slightly resembled the same mousy, unassuming girl she'd once been. "She was nice-looking, yes. I never really noticed." He winced, realizing how horrible that made him sound, especially since they'd created a child together.

"Tell me about her."

"Don't do this," he begged.

"I need to know, Cole. If I'm going to make sense out of this—"

"You can't," he interrupted harshly. "You can't rationalize an irrational decision. God knows I've tried."

"Maybe I can't, but I need to know who she was, what she was like. Why she could help you sort out your problems but I couldn't."

Her quiet, almost defeated tone convinced him to dredge up his memories in order to reassure her. "She didn't compare to you, in looks or temperament. She was…different from the other girls."

She flopped onto her back. "Different how?"

He sighed, sensing she wouldn't rest until he told her what she wanted to know—whatever that was. "She tended to be a spectator, a bystander if you will, rather than a participant, which meant she'd faded into the background. Ruth got shuffled from foster home to foster home, so she didn't trust many people. Only a few of us got to see the real Ruth—the Ruth who could crack

jokes with a straight face, the Ruth who'd do anything for a friend if it was within her power. She'd
helped me with my senior English project—we
had to create a papier-mâché character from
Beowulf—and I was all thumbs when it came to
art. To repay her, I took her to the senior prom
because I knew she was dying to go but no one
had asked her."

Sara turned to face him, which was promising,
in his opinion. "I didn't know you ever went to
your prom."

"Yeah, well, it wasn't important enough to mention." Suddenly aware that he'd recited that same
excuse throughout his entire life when anyone
asked about his past, he winced.

"So what did you wear?"

She clearly wanted to know every detail. "After
four months of saving my money, I rented a tux,"
he admitted. "Ruth found a bright pink dress that
made her look like a bottle of stomach medicine,
but it had all this glittery stuff on it and crinkled
when she walked. She said that even though it
came from a secondhand shop, she felt like a
fairy-tale princess."

"What happened to her parents?"

"I'm not really sure," he said. "She'd mentioned

living with a grandmother and after she died, Ruth went into foster care."

"No aunts or uncles or siblings?"

"I don't think so, at least none that she ever talked about. I'm sure if there'd been a relative, social services would have located them."

She fell silent for a minute. "What happened after high school?"

"Our paths didn't cross. Occasionally, I'd hear what she was doing, but Ruth didn't stay in touch and I didn't expect her to. She'd wanted to forget her childhood and everything associated with it. I didn't blame her. We were both biding our time until we finished school and could leave and be on our own."

"Yet she came to your reunion."

"Yeah, it was the first one she'd ever attended. As I said before, I was surprised when I saw her."

For the longest time, he waited for her to speak again. When she didn't, even though he hated to break their uneasy truce, he had to.

"What did you think of Brody?" he asked.

She sighed. "He's a cute kid and obviously very intelligent, too. He looks a lot like you."

He pictured his son's face and felt an odd sense of male pride, which was quite amazing when he considered how a few short years ago he hadn't planned to get married, much less have a family. "Do you think so?"

"Oh, yes. Definitely. Were you as busy a fellow as he was?"

"I don't remember," he said honestly. Sadly enough, he had no one to ask, either. "I imagine I was, though."

He felt her nod. "That's how I pictured you, too. Speaking of pictures, do you have any of you as a child?"

Cole thought of the shoebox tucked away on the top shelf of his closet, buried behind an odd collection of off-season clothing and Sara's handbags. "A few," he said.

"Will you show them to me?"

Somehow, it had always seemed safer to keep those photos—and the memories—locked away, but if Sara had her way, he'd eventually bring them into the open.

"Yeah, sure. Sometime," he said, because refusing wouldn't help his cause and if fate was kind, she'd forget she'd asked. Then, because the suspense was killing him, he asked, "Have you thought about Ruth's request?"

"Yes."

He allowed the pause to last for a full minute before he prompted her to continue. "And?"

"I saw the way you looked at him," she said simply. "You want him, don't you?"

He'd tried to hide his feelings—and his potential disappointment—but Sara clearly knew him too well. Although he felt completely inadequate to be a parent and hated the emotional cost she would pay for his past actions, he couldn't deny that he wanted the privilege of raising Brody.

"Did you think I wouldn't?" he asked instead.

She sighed. "No. I would have been worried if you didn't."

It occurred to him that his reaction could represent another difference between him and his relatives... Somehow, he felt as if he'd passed a test that he hadn't realized he'd been taking.

"And yet," she continued, "when we talked about having a baby of our own, you didn't seem as eager."

How could he explain that while he wanted to have a baby with Sara because he loved her, in the back of his mind his less-than-admirable role models had made him reluctant to embrace the idea with Sara's degree of enthusiasm?

"Just because I was happy to take things slow

didn't mean I wasn't eager," he pointed out. "Besides, you can't compare us having our own baby to present circumstances. What we're facing now isn't the ideal way to start our family, but it's the situation we have to deal with."

Slowly, she nodded. For a few seconds they both lay in silence until she finally spoke with resignation in her voice.

"We don't have a choice, do we? He *is* your son, and as you said, he doesn't have anyone else."

"Yes, he's mine, but our decision can't be based on *obligation.* If that's how you feel, then this won't work," he finished flatly. As a child, he'd learned quickly how uncomfortable it was being treated as an "obligation" rather than a member of a family.

Her eyebrows drew together. "I don't feel obligated, but as your wife I suppose I feel a sense of responsibility, even if I'm not completely sold on the idea. At least not yet," she tacked on. "So if you're expecting me to jump up and down with excitement about bringing him into our home, you'll be sorely disappointed. However, I know that we're both too softhearted to live with the idea of giving him up."

He suspected as much and, in fact, her admission was more than he'd allowed himself to hope for. Somehow he sensed a smile wouldn't be appreciated, so he simply nodded to acknowledge her decision.

"Softhearted or not, I appreciate your willingness to welcome him here. I can't imagine trying to raise him without you."

For a man who'd learned to hide weakness and hated to reveal an insecurity, he was almost surprised he had. Sara, however, didn't seem to take his comment as a confession. Instead, it was as if she suspected he was only paying her a compliment to make this bitter pill more palatable to swallow.

"With or without me, I think you can do whatever you put your mind to doing," she told him evenly.

"Oh, Sara…" He leaned over and kissed her, noticing how she held herself stiffly under his caress.

"I know how difficult this is for you," he began contritely, "but everything will work out."

"I hope so, Cole."

Her packed suitcase and his probationary status indicated as much. The truth was, he wasn't confident at all. Brody's presence would remind her of the baby they'd lost and of the baby she was trying so hard to create, so she'd need time—and love—to recover.

"I'll do my best to convince you," he promised. "You won't regret doing this for Brody or for us, Sara."

She sighed. "I just don't want to compound one mistake with another."

He couldn't agree more. "As long as we pull together, we'll make it work."

CHAPTER THREE

WHEN Sara padded into the kitchen at seven-thirty the next morning, wearing her nightgown and robe, she found the coffee ready and Cole seated at the table. His mug was half-empty and the top page of a legal pad full of nearly illegible handwriting lay in front of him.

"Good morning," he said cautiously, as if he suspected from the way she'd tossed and turned all night that she wasn't disposed to doling out forgiveness just yet.

"Morning," she mumbled as she poured a mug for herself. "How long have you been awake?"

"A couple of hours," he admitted. "I couldn't sleep, thinking of everything we have to do today. So I got up and made a list."

She hadn't been able to sleep, either, although she couldn't claim the same excuse. Her thoughts had lingered along the lines of trying to work out how she was going to be the mother that Brody so obviously needed when the idea of inflicting a few medieval tortures on his father held immense appeal.

By 2:00 a.m., though, she'd gotten past her thirst for bodily harm and she'd started to look at her situation with a little more objectivity. The hurt was still there, as well as the disappointment over his one-night stand—even if it had occurred while they'd been separated—but, as Cole had said, their time together over the past six years had been good. He deserved credit for that.

A little credit, anyway.

And maybe, someday, she would be able to trust him again. At the moment, the man she'd thought she'd known seemed like a stranger.

As for Brody and the task she'd accepted, she simply had to think of him as a motherless little boy with no one to take him in. A motherless little boy who needed someone, namely her, to assume his mother's role.

Unfortunately, it wouldn't be easy because he resembled Cole in such a painfully obvious manner. She'd have to train her thoughts to not go down that fruitless path, just as she'd have to train herself not to wonder if he was still unable to share his fears with her and if he had any other secrets that would eventually haunt them.

Idly, she wondered how long it would take before those thoughts of Brody became second nature because right now they were not. In any case, Cole was studying her with cautious optimism as if hoping she'd already forgiven and forgotten, which meant it was time to begin that painful process.

She forced herself to sit beside him at the table when she'd rather take her coffee into the other room to drink in peace. "What's on your to-do list?"

"First was to cancel our plane tickets and our hotel reservation, which I've already done."

Although she'd known it had been inevitable, a fresh pang of disappointment struck. "That was fast," she commented before she, without thinking, sipped on her hot coffee and burned the roof of her mouth in the process.

"I'm sorry about this weekend, but I promise we'll go another time."

But it won't be the same, she wanted to cry, before she realized that given these events and her shattered feelings, celebrating their anniversary as if their lives hadn't taken a right turn seemed hypocritical.

"Yeah, sure. Another time," she echoed, wondering if another anniversary was actually *in* their future.

"I mean it," he insisted, as if he sensed her doubts. "I'll make it up to you."

"Fine." Then, because she wanted to push that subject aside before she embarrassed herself with tears, she asked, "What else is on the list?"

He shoved the pad closer to her. "Childproof the house, which means we have to put away all the things he might destroy, like your figurines. Then we need to install latches on the drawers and cupboard doors that we don't want him to open, which means a trip to the hardware store. The unused electrical outlets need plugs, too, which is something else we have to buy."

She perused the list, impressed by his thoroughness. Then again, he'd been at this for hours. "You've given this a lot of thought."

He shrugged. "I tried, but I'm hoping you'll notice something I've missed."

"It looks rather complete to me."

He glanced at the clock. "It's nearly eight. I thought I'd call the Maitlands while you're getting dressed and then we'll run to the store before they arrive."

"Slow down a minute," she said. "I know how

eager you are, but they might be sleeping in. Absolutely do *not* call them before nine."

He frowned, then his expression turned sheepish. "You're right. Nine o'clock is early enough. Do you think we can drive to the hardware store and back before then?"

"Is that a hint I should hurry and get dressed?" she asked wryly.

He chuckled. "It is."

While she showered and dressed, hurrying because his impatience was so obvious, she reminded herself not to look on the situation with dread but with anticipation. Even though the child she'd been hoping, praying and waiting for wasn't coming in the way she'd envisioned, one was coming nonetheless. The only way they could make this work was to pull together, as Cole had said last night.

As it turned out, Cole didn't phone the Maitlands until almost nine-thirty. After that, they worked feverishly to accomplish as many projects on Cole's list as possible before their guests arrived at eleven.

After Cole had dropped a screw several times while he was trying to install a latch on a cabinet door, Sara smiled at her husband's uncharacteristic clumsiness, wishing for an instant that the anxiety—and suppressed excitement—she'd seen all morning had been for *her* child, and not Ruth's. Unfortunately, it didn't accomplish anything for her thoughts to dwell there, so she pushed them aside.

It was a sad day when every thought had to be discarded…

"Nervous?" she asked.

He looked up at her and grinned sheepishly. "Does it show?"

"A little," she admitted.

He sat back on his heels. "This all seems so surreal. As a physician, I'm used to juggling responsibilities for my patients, from making a diagnosis to choosing the best treatment option, and yet the idea of being responsible for one little boy is…" He shrugged, as if unable to find the right word.

"Overwhelming? Daunting? Frightening?" she supplied.

"All that and more," he answered. "None of that hit me until I started looking at all the possible ways a child could hurt himself around here." He glanced around the kitchen, his expression rueful. "I'd always preached safety to parents and felt rather smug about it, but now that *I'm* standing on the other side, knowing *I'm* the one who has to have eyes in the back of my head and practice what I've always preached, it's a different story."

"We'll definitely have a steep learning curve," she said.

He studied her for a moment. "What about you? Are you nervous?"

She paused to consider. "A little," she finally answered. "As you said, this is a huge responsibility. Normally we'd have nine months to get used to the idea of being parents and to physically prepare. Instead, we've gotten twenty-four hours. Less than that, actually."

He nodded, then met her gaze. "Have you told your parents?"

"Heavens, no. Not yet." She'd thought about phoning them, but hadn't arrived at a way to explain the situation without making Cole look bad. Another wife facing these circumstances might not care, but for reasons she couldn't pinpoint, *she* did. Suggesting to her parents that she hadn't known Cole as well as she'd thought she had didn't slide down well at all.

"If you don't mind, when you're ready, *I'll* break the news to them," he declared.

His offer took her by surprise before she realized it required both guts and a strong dose of humility to face his in-laws and admit to actions that didn't show him in the best light.

Silently, she added several points into his plus column. If he could brave the wrath of her mother and father, then he was obviously willing to accept whatever penance they doled out.

But penance or not, the fact remained that he'd kept so much of his life hidden, even from her, and she begged to know why. It wasn't for lack of asking, because she had. The most he'd told her was that he'd moved in with his aunt and uncle after his parents had died, and that those times had not been happy ones. Because he'd treated those questions with easy nonchalance, she'd assumed his life had been filled with the usual teenage problems and angst with nothing remarkable to note.

Now she suspected otherwise. Now she suspected that those days had been so traumatic that he refused to revisit them. It would certainly explain why she'd never met any of his relatives, even at their wedding.

But, she vowed to herself, the time for secrets was over. She wanted to know *precisely* what experiences had shaped Cole into the man he was. Dredging up bad memories wouldn't be pleasant, but it was necessary. While this particular minute wasn't the appropriate time to ask those questions, those days would be discussed.

Soon.

She shook her head. "We'll tell my parents together. Knowing my mother, she'll be thrilled to have a grandbaby, especially this close to Christmas. My dad will be happy, too, *after* he delivers his famous right hook. And after my brothers throw a few punches of their own."

A ghost of a smile appeared on his face. "I figured as much." He met her gaze. "What about you? How are you holding up?"

Like I'm being held together with a wad of used-up chewing gum, she wanted to say. Instead, she answered, "Fine."

His gaze landed on her arms crossed protectively over her chest and she dropped them to her sides. "Really?" he asked.

"Yes," she said more firmly than she felt. It was pointless to belabor how her biggest problem came when she thought of how Brody was more Cole's than hers. While Cole only saw Brody's arrival as the beginning of a wonderful future with his own flesh and blood, she saw it as the beginning of an extremely difficult emotional journey.

"If I could relive that weekend, I would. I wish I'd never gone," he added fiercely.

"Don't apologize again, Cole. I know you're sorry and, as you said, technically we were both free to…see…other people during that time."

She wished she hadn't been so delighted to see him when he'd appeared on her doorstep after their ten-day separation. In fact, she'd been so thrilled by his declaration that he'd been miserable without her that she hadn't bothered to ask questions. Instead, she'd assumed he'd been sitting at home every night, alone and lonely, just as she had been.

That was the problem with assuming.

However, she couldn't correct that mistake now.

"I'm still trying to sort out everything," she continued honestly. "One day, I hope I'll be as thrilled with Brody as you are, but it won't be today."

He nodded, as if he accepted her terms. "I don't want him to pay for my mistake."

"Regardless of what you've done, I wouldn't make a child become your scapegoat," she chided, suddenly realizing that Cole had his own trust issues to work on.

He shrugged. "One never knows how another person will react when the chips are down."

Part of her wondered what had happened during his childhood and the other part was irritated that after a six-year relationship, he still questioned her character.

She poked him in the chest. "You can take what I said to the bank," she said fervently. "I haven't broken a vow to you yet, have I?"

"No," he said slowly.

"Then consider what I just said to be a new vow. I won't hold Brody accountable for your actions. He's an innocent little boy and it isn't his fault how he came to exist."

He nodded, as if satisfied she meant what she'd said. "Okay."

The doorbell chimes sounded and she exchanged a glance with him. "They're here," she said inanely, feeling her heart skip a beat.

As she met Cole's gaze in that instant, the realization of what she'd agreed to came crashing down. A combination of dread and excitement caused her to take Cole's hand. They still had a lot of personal issues to deal with, but they were in this new venture of raising Brody together.

Cole squeezed Sara's hand, grateful that in spite of the problems in their relationship, she had reached out to him in this moment.

That alone gave him hope that they'd eventually be able to repair the damage. Working on that restoration, however, would have to wait for another time. Right now, they had the more immediate task of welcoming the Maitlands inside.

"Brr, it's gotten cold early this year," Parker said, stamping his feet. "I'm thinking we'll have a white Christmas."

While he and Cole discussed Parker's prediction and a long-term weather forecast, Cole's gaze never left his son. He watched as young Brody ripped his stocking hat off his head and his mittens off his hands. His coat was closed with snaps and in a flash he ripped them apart and his royal-blue parka had landed on the floor.

Eloise stared at him fondly as she handed her own knee-length leather coat to Sara. "That boy," she said with a trace of exasperation. "Before you know it, his shoes will be off, too."

She'd hardly finished speaking when Brody plopped onto the floor, twisted off his shoes and stared at the grown-ups, looking pleased at his accomplishment.

Eloise shook her head. "Just like his mother."

Like a sudden, noxious fume, her words hung in the air and Cole hated seeing Sara's response. For an instant, a stricken expression crossed her features, which made Cole wish he had the ability to erase Eloise's thoughtless remark. Fortunately, Eloise took matters into her own hands.

"I'm sorry, dear," the woman said softly, her face pink with obvious embarrassment. "My observation just slipped out. It's just that Ruth was like our own daughter. I still can't believe she's gone."

"Don't give it another thought," Sara said magnanimously, but Cole saw her brittle smile, knew how much her gesture cost and felt a now-familiar ache of regret and sorrow lodge in his chest.

"Naturally, he'll have some of her traits," Sara continued. "Ignoring them doesn't change the facts. I'm sure you have a lot of things to tell us, so please sit down."

"Yes, please do," Cole echoed, once again mentally telegraphing his apologies to his wife.

"Brody?" Eloise chided as she did. "Please pick up your coat and give it to your daddy."

Daddy. The sound of his new title came as a blow to his solar plexus. Was this how his own father had felt when *he* had been born? Had he been as overwhelmed by the responsibility as *he* now was? But as the little boy shyly glanced at Cole, that panicky feeling slowly transformed into a firm resolve to handle the job to the best of his ability.

Brody clearly didn't have the same conflicting emotions to sort through because he simply smiled before he thrust his coat into Cole's hands. Without hesitation and clearly without dwelling on the ramifications that having a father would mean for him, Brody brushed past Sara and grabbed the oversize bag that Eloise had carried inside. With a herculean effort on his part, he hauled the sack to Cole and dumped it at his feet. "Toys."

Realizing his son had taken the news in his stride, Cole laughed with some relief that the little boy didn't sense his new father's insecurities. "Are you asking me to play?"

Immediately Brody bobbed his head and began pulling out cars and trucks, a container of blocks and an assortment of other colorful items.

"We brought his favorites," Parker said as he sat on the sofa beside his wife.

"Including his teddy bear," Eloise said. "A word of warning—do not lose that bear. It's his bed-time buddy."

"That's good to know."

Suddenly, Brody tugged on Cole's fingers. "Daddy, play," he demanded. "Box."

As the child grabbed the drawstring bag containing his blocks, Cole sat on the floor beside him, overjoyed to hear that one word coming from his son's mouth. "Okay," he said agreeably, "we'll stack blocks."

As Sara watched the two build a tower that eventually leaned, then crashed to Brody's delight, the sight of the two dark heads together was a bittersweet moment.

He should have been their *son.*

The fact that he wasn't bothered her more than anything else. She still wasn't happy about so many things but being around his child only emphasized how after a miscarriage and subsequent months of trying to get pregnant again, nothing had happened on that front. Although Cole had suggested waiting for Josh's recommended year to pass before going ahead for fertility tests, she had suddenly become too impatient. If there was truly a problem of some sort, she wanted to know now, rather than later. After all, what difference would a few months make?

Of course, to get pregnant, she couldn't keep to her side of the bed every night and she wasn't ready to cross the center line. Her emotions were too raw and her faith too crushed to entertain the idea, which meant her wish for a special Christmas present wouldn't happen. She wanted to howl out her grief for that setback, too, but now wasn't the time or the place.

For the next ten minutes, Cole played with his son while Sara stoically listened to the information that Eloise and Parker freely shared. She really should write their tips down, she decided, because at the moment, her brain felt like a sieve.

Finally, the youngster rose from his kneeling position and hurried over to Eloise.

"Dwink," he demanded.

"Ask your Mama Sara," Eloise encouraged.

He cocked his head and his face grew thoughtful. "Mama?"

Eloise pointed to Sara. "Sara is your new mama," she told him. "Ask her. Ask Mama Sara."

He stared at Sara, the wrinkle between his little

eyebrows revealing that he didn't understand how this was possible. "No." He shook his head before glancing around the room. "Want *my* mama."

As he looked back at Sara, his face wrinkled with unhappiness and he burst into tears. "Mama," he cried, crawling into Eloise's lap.

Although Sara hadn't expected Brody to accept her easily, his rejection bothered her more than she'd thought it might. "Please don't push the issue," she said.

"I'm so sorry, dear," Eloise apologized as she cuddled Brody. "I'm not doing a very good job with this transition, am I? It was thoughtless of me and I should have known... I've been trying to tell him that you're his new mother, and I thought that by tacking on your name, he'd accept the change, but he doesn't seem to understand."

"I'm sure he doesn't," Sara said, feeling sorry for the child who was faithfully waiting for the most important person in his young life to reappear. The ironic thing was that she'd been worried about how *she'd* accept being his mother when she should have been more concerned about Brody accepting *her*.

"He knows what he called his mother," she pointed out, "and adding another name is probably confusing him. All things considered, he should probably think of me as Sara for now. It'll be less stressful."

"You're probably right, dear," Eloise said as she kissed Brody's forehead and smoothed his hair.

Wondering how long it would take for Brody to turn to *her* for comfort instead of seeing her as the enemy, Sara rose. Perhaps if she left the room, Brody would calm down. "I'll get him a cup of juice," she mentioned to no one in particular. "And coffee for the rest of us."

As Brody's wails increased in volume, she fled to the kitchen and began preparing a tray.

"Need help?" Cole asked a few minutes later.

She brushed past him to remove the creamer from the refrigerator, refusing to meet his gaze and see the pity in his eyes. "No, thanks. I can manage."

He grabbed her arm and tethered her in place. "He doesn't understand, Sara."

She wasn't ready to accept his comfort and she stiffened. "Don't you think I know that?" she asked.

To her surprise, as if he'd decided he wouldn't be rejected so easily, he didn't release his grip. "He'll come around."

"Sure he will," she dutifully agreed. *Maybe when he's eighteen.*

"He will," he insisted. "He'll soon learn what I've known for a long time…that you're a kind and loving person who has a heart big enough to let him in, no matter what."

"Stop trying to flatter me."

"This isn't flattery. It's the truth. I may not be a psychiatrist, but this isn't a rejection of you. He's frustrated because his life has crumbled around him and he doesn't understand why or know how to repair it."

Boy, could she relate to that!

She sighed. Young Brody had to learn how to make the best of an uncomfortable situation just as she did. She might not share a blood bond with the child, but they certainly shared this emotional one.

"I know," she agreed. "As Parker told us last night, the adjustment won't happen overnight."

Slowly, Cole's hold became more of a caress than a leash, making her realize how much she'd missed the closeness of their physical contact and she'd only done without for less than twenty-four hours. Yet, she wasn't quite ready to forgive him, even if he was being thoughtful and supportive.

"Dwink," she heard a plaintive voice demand loudly in the other room.

Brody's request broke the mood of the moment and she tugged free of Cole's hand. "Would you mind carrying in Brody's juice? I'll bring the coffee in a minute."

He nodded, then left with the plastic cup she'd poured.

As Sara lifted the tray and prepared to follow him, the incident painfully reminded her that she wasn't Brody's mother. She knew it and the sad thing was that little Brody knew it, too.

CHAPTER FOUR

THE time with the Maitlands went all too quickly and before Cole knew it, he and Sara were on their own. Fortunately, both of them had received short-term compassionate leave so Brody wouldn't have to attend day care just yet, but Cole knew those two weeks would flash by.

After only three days of being a parent, Cole had decided that a hectic day at the hospital was less exhausting than following this little whirlwind of energy. At the same time, though, these new experiences were energizing. They also reminded him of all the usual milestones he'd missed—first steps, first smiles, first words. He hated that those were memories he could never recover, but he was also grateful that he'd stand nearby for the subsequent ones.

At the moment, though, the tense moments were balancing out the good ones. He'd caught himself on several occasions thoughtlessly commenting on Brody's habits that were so characteristic of his mother, like kicking off his shoes whenever he could.

As if Sara had needed a reminder that Brody wasn't hers, he'd scolded himself. Although she had nodded and gone about her business, Cole had seen the bleakness in her eyes in spite of the smile she'd pasted on her face. Gut-wrenching guilt had swept over him for his insensitivity and the urge to fall back into old habits and look for a means of escape sounded more and more attractive. He'd been tempted to call the Maitlands on more than one occasion and announce that they'd changed their minds—that having Brody around was as painful as probing an open wound, that he simply couldn't subject his wife to such misery—but he never acted on those thoughts. For one thing, it was cowardly to use Sara as his excuse when she hadn't uttered one word of complaint.

Neither was he the ten-year-old boy who'd clung to the only hope he'd had—the hope that one day his life would no longer be subject to the whims of others. He'd grown up with one goal in mind—to endure as best he could, while vowing to never be placed in a similar situation.

Sadly, that mindset had nearly cost him Sara.

It seemed as if his present circumstances were another test that the fates had decided to give in order to see if he was willing to face a few more of his deep-seated fears. While escape seemed attractive at times, it really wasn't an option—not if he wanted to keep any measure of self-respect.

Then there were the moments when Brody's mannerisms mirrored his and he saw himself in the youngster's features. How could he possibly give up the privilege of raising his own son?

Those feelings were reinforced whenever Brody came to him without hesitation or fear. Without any muss or fuss, Brody had accepted him as his father and their relationship was already growing by leaps and bounds, probably because he was still trying to sort out what role a father played in his young life when he'd never had one before.

Unfortunately, Sara wasn't faring as well. Although she'd said several times that she wasn't taking Brody's rejection to heart, Cole suspected the little boy's wariness troubled her. Normally, children gravitated to her, but ever since Eloise had referred to her as "Mama," Brody had stared at her with suspicion and only went to her when no one else was available.

Cole had tried to stand in the gap, but he suspected he wasn't doing a stellar job. While he told the youngster that Sara hadn't been responsible for his mother's disappearance, he wasn't sure that Brody understood. Somehow, he had to figure out a way to persuade the little boy that Sara hadn't created this sudden gaping hole in his short life, but so far he'd drawn a blank.

It wasn't the only blank he was drawing, either. Their anniversary was coming up soon and he still didn't know how they could celebrate the occasion. Dinner at the fanciest restaurant in town ranked high on his list, but he couldn't figure out the logistics. He might still be finding his way when it came to juggling the roles of parent and husband, but he instinctively knew that bringing Brody with them defeated the purpose of giving his wife his full and undivided attention. One of his colleagues had mentioned how he and his wife had kept a date night to keep their romance fresh after the kids had started to arrive, and he couldn't think of a better time to start the habit than with their anniversary. Unfortunately, hiring a sitter for the evening was out of the question. Brody didn't need another stranger introduced into his life so soon after moving in with a couple he'd only known a few weeks.

Of course they could always postpone their celebration until their life with Brody settled into a routine, but that could take months. Sara would probably understand if their special day passed without their usual fanfare, but Cole didn't *want* her to have to understand. He wanted her to know that she was still number one in his life. He simply needed to be creative. Luckily, he still had about ten days to dream up the perfect celebration.

As he mentally considered his options and scanned the newspaper's business ads, Brody climbed onto his lap as he clutched one of his cars. "Daddy, wet."

"That's nice," Cole murmured idly, his thoughts still focused on creating the perfect anniversary celebration.

Brody babbled something that Cole couldn't understand, but as he dropped the newspaper to listen, he suddenly became aware of a dampness seeping into his jeans.

"Are you wet, Brody?" he asked.

"Wet," the little boy echoed as he enthusiastically bobbed his head.

Suddenly, Cole realized that he'd never dealt with Brody's basic needs since he'd come to live with them. While he was willing to do his share, he also realized that he'd never changed a diaper before in his life. He didn't have the first idea of how to go about it.

"Okay, bud," he said as he rose and took Brody's hand. "Shall we see if Sara will help us out this time?"

He led Brody to the kitchen, where Sara was drying dishes. She paused, tea towel in hand. "If you're here to beg for more cookies, the answer is no. We just had lunch."

He grinned. "As wonderful as another cookie sounds, we're not here for that. Brody needs his britches changed."

Sara met his gaze. "Then change him. You can take off his clothes and put on a fresh diaper as well as I can."

"But I've never diapered before," he protested.

"There's no time like the present to learn," she said smartly.

"I've never even *seen* it done." He hoped that would sway the argument in his favor. "Can you show me? For Brody's sake?"

For a minute, she looked as if she might refuse, but then her shoulders slumped in an obvious sign of capitulation. She tossed the towel onto the counter and shooed them ahead of her to Brody's bedroom where she proceeded to stand back and supervise while Cole pulled off Brody's pants.

"All you have to do is pay attention when you remove the wet one," she said as he ripped off the tapes holding the soggy diaper around Brody's waist. "Then put the new one on."

Cole followed her instructions as she watched, feeling as clumsy as the first time he'd sutured a gash under the critical eye of his professor.

"Shouldn't he be toilet trained by now?" he asked, desperately hoping this stage would soon fall behind them.

"Eloise said that Ruth had started to work with him, but she hadn't gotten very far."

"Then maybe we should make that a priority."

"You're welcome to try," she answered cheerfully, "but until he adjusts to his new circumstances, I think it best if we wait awhile. Even if we started immediately, it won't fix Brody's immediate problem. So resign yourself to changing a few diapers. Just be glad he's only wet."

Now, *that* was a scenario Cole hoped he'd never have to face by himself.

In the end, the entire process was far less stressful than Cole had expected.

"Will you two be okay by yourselves while I run a few errands this afternoon?" she asked.

It would be the first time Cole had been completely alone with Brody without Sara for backup. While he knew that day had to come, he wasn't ready to face it just yet, which was an odd thing for a man who'd gone through medical school and an internal medicine residency to fear, he thought wryly.

"Why don't we go with you?" he asked instead.

Sara paused. "It's really cold to be taking him outside unnecessarily," she began.

"We're driving, not walking," he pointed out. "And we'll warm the car before we go. He'll be fine. Besides, it'll be fun."

"Fun?" She stared at him as if he'd grown another nose. "You clearly haven't shopped with a toddler before."

"I haven't," he admitted, "but how hard can it be with both of us?"

An hour later, Cole's words of *how hard can it be?* came back to haunt him. He could explain in vivid detail of how difficult it was to keep one active, curious toddler occupied while taking care of the business of shopping.

Fortunately, Sara didn't say "I told you so."

Instead, she simply smiled and suggested that he concentrate on his son while she filled the cart with the essentials.

So Cole obliged. At first it wasn't too difficult to entertain the little boy as he sat in the cart, but that soon grew boring.

"At the risk of making a huge mistake," Cole said as Brody kicked his legs and arched his back to try and escape his seat, "maybe he'd be less noisy if I let him walk."

"Do you really think you can hold on to him?" Sara asked. "If he darts away…"

"I'll hold his hand," he said as he lifted the youngster out of the cart.

"You'd better," she said darkly.

Freed from his constraints, Brody clung to Cole's hand until he suddenly jumped up and down with obvious delight. "Toys!" he squealed, before slipping out of Cole's grasp and racing toward every child's favorite section of a store.

Fear struck Cole's gut. Although he was never more than two steps behind his son, the idea that his little boy was quicker than he was gave him new sympathy for parents whose children darted into harm's way while under their watchful eye. By the time he'd toyed with the idea of tethering

Brody to him until he was at least sixteen, he'd caught up to him.

Brody, with reflexes as quick as any pickpocket's, had snatched a stuffed lion off the shelf and wrapped both arms around it. He talked to the lion as if it were his long-lost pal.

"What did you find, Brody?" Cole asked.

"Grr," Brody said. "Wions grr."

Like all parents, Cole was impressed with his son's obvious knowledge. "Yes, lions growl."

The little boy nodded. "Grr."

Cole glanced at Sara, who'd finally caught up with them. "Smart kid," he said proudly. "Who would have thought a stuffed lion would catch his eye?"

"Who would have thought," she echoed, looking both relieved and exasperated. "Unfortunately, as much fun as it is to stay and play, I have everything on my list."

Cole spoke to Brody. "Okay, son. Put down the lion. It's time to leave."

Brody shook his head and clutched the toy to his chest. "No."

"Yes," he said firmly.

"No-o-o-o," the toddler yelled as Cole reached for the toy. "Mine."

"It's not yours," Cole said patiently.

Brody frowned. "Mine."

"Brody," Cole said sternly. "We have to leave the lion."

Brody's lower lip quivered and a huge tear slid down his cheek as he continued to hug the lion. "Mine," he sniffled. "My wion."

Although Cole knew that giving in to tears didn't bode well for the future, Brody's obvious distress tugged at his sympathies. Unsure of what to do, he glanced at Sara and shrugged helplessly, hoping she'd give him some direction on how to handle Brody's tantrum.

Sara saw Cole's indecisiveness and knew he wanted her to intervene. The resentful, still hurting side of her insisted that she let him deal with the situation on his own—after all, he'd wanted to be a parent and she was struggling with her own feelings of inadequacy, so why shouldn't he?—but one thought after another popped into her head and made her repent.

I can't do this without you, Sara.

Brody is yours, too.

She'd stepped into Ruth's shoes, albeit reluctantly, but an agreement was an agreement. She needed to fulfill her part of this bargain and if the truth were known, she wasn't immune to Brody's obvious distress, either. However, before she could offer a suggestion, Cole crouched beside the youngster, held out his hand and spoke softly, yet firmly.

"Brody, give me the toy."

"Daddy, *mine,*" Brody wailed. "Warry is my wion."

"This lion isn't yours," Cole explained with surprising patience.

Suddenly, Sara understood what was happening. She placed a hand on Cole's shoulder. "You don't suppose he has a stuffed lion like this one, do you? It would explain why he thinks this is his."

Cole stared up at her. "He could just be throwing the usual two-year-old temper tantrum."

Sara glanced at Brody and watched as he buried his nose in the lion's neck. "He might," she admitted, "but I don't think he is. He called the lion Larry. What child his age names a toy in less than five minutes?"

Cole hesitated as he obviously mulled over Sara's comment.

"Even if he is acting like a normal toddler who wants what catches his eye," Sara continued, "after all the adjustments he's been forced to cope with lately, do you really want to deny him this one small thing just to prove a point or establish that you're the boss?"

The little boy's soulful gaze would have melted Sara's heart even if she hadn't connected the dots about the lion and it obviously had the same effect on Cole because a look of relief spread across his face, which suggested that he hadn't wanted to disappoint the little boy but had thought he'd had to.

He rose, plucking Brody and his lion off the floor in one smooth motion. "Okay, sprout. Let's take Larry the lion home."

This time, Brody didn't fuss as Cole settled him back in the cart. Instead, he bestowed such a huge smile on his father—a smile of gratefulness that was only more powerful because of the tears glimmering in his eyes—that Sara sensed she'd read the situation correctly.

Over the next few hours, Sara watched Brody shower attention on his lion. She'd obviously done something right for the boy, which made her rethink her ability to act as his mother. Granted, what she'd done was minor in the grand scheme of things, but it pleased her to know that she'd been able to put her personal issues aside—for a short time, at least—to focus on Brody. Maybe, given enough time, she *could* be the mother he needed her to be.

Now she had to focus on trying to be the wife that she still was... It wasn't easy. The hurt was still there and it showed in their stilted conversations—conversations that centered around Brody to the exclusion of all else.

It would take more time than had passed so far for her to return to their former easiness but, strained relations or not, she was still observant. And she'd observed that her husband, who wasn't a talkative man on any given day, seemed more introspective than usual.

She sensed it had to do with their trip to the store—maybe he was still fighting the same heart-stopping fear that she had when Brody bolted out of reach—but she waited for him to speak.

As the late-afternoon shadows began to lengthen, she decided enough was enough. While there were still many topics that she considered off-limits, they had to start communicating about *something*. Discussing Cole's current feelings seemed like a good place to start.

As she watched Brody drive his lion across the living room floor in his largest dump truck, she was certain the right moment had arrived when Cole finally joined them.

"I just phoned the Maitlands," he said offhand-edly before she could broach the subject on her mind.

"What for?"

"To satisfy my curiosity. It seems Brody *does* have a stuffed lion but Eloise said he didn't play with it very often, so she didn't bring it with him. It's boxed with the rest of his things that should arrive any day now."

Sara smiled, inordinately pleased by his announcement. "I wonder what he'll say when he realizes he now has *two* Larrys."

"Yeah, I wonder." He fell silent for a few seconds. "How did you know it was so important to him?" he asked.

She shrugged. "I didn't. I watched, listened and had a hunch. That's all."

"Yeah, well, your hunch seems fairly accurate. Obviously the conclusion I drew was way off base."

She heard the disgust in his voice. From personal experience, she recognized his suffering as a bout of perceived failure and while part of her wanted him to stew over it, she simply couldn't let it happen. Not because she was feeling particularly benevolent but because he was her husband, and she still hated to see him hurting.

"Don't be so hard on yourself," she told him. "You were only trying to do what any parent would do under the circumstances."

"Maybe, but you were obviously more attuned to the situation than I was. I didn't hear him call the toy by name, but you did."

"Only because I was the objective bystander and you weren't."

"Maybe, but what happens next time, especially if I'm by myself and don't have your powers of observation? This is exactly—"

He stopped short and Sara waited for him to continue. "Exactly what?" she prompted.

He hesitated.

"This is exactly *what,* Cole?" she repeated.

"It's what I was afraid of," he burst out. "Being inadequate. Maybe I'm not cut out to be a father."

"You aren't the only one who suffers from doubts," she pointed out. "My dad always said that anyone who isn't daunted by the responsibility of parenthood has an overinflated view of himself. The question is, do you still *want* to be a father?"

He nodded.

"Then stop worrying about making a mistake. If there's a repeat of today's incident at the store, you'll make the best decision based on the circumstances at the time," she said simply. "Sometimes we'll get it right, like we did today, and sometimes we won't. Parenthood isn't a perfect science."

His chuckle was weak. "No kidding."

"The point is, the more we get to know Brody, the easier it'll be to tell the difference between a tantrum and when he's truly upset about something."

He nodded slowly before his gaze grew speculative. "Thanks for the pep talk."

Given that their relationship was still broken and that she hadn't been able to dole out any forgiveness yet, his gratitude made her a little uncomfortable. "It was nothing," she said, dismissing him with a breezy wave of her hands.

"Thanks also for not saying 'I told you so.' Shopping with a toddler isn't as easy as it sounds," he added ruefully.

"It isn't," she agreed. Then, because she was

curious, she asked, "Would you have felt better if I had?"

"No, but you would have had the satisfaction. It was a perfect opportunity for you to point out how inexperienced and unqualified I am."

"It would have been," she admitted, "but all first-time parents are inexperienced until time solves that problem. Besides, what purpose would it have served?"

"You'd have felt vindicated."

"Maybe, but, again, how would that have helped either of us?" she asked, fully aware that the urge to do just that hadn't completely left her. She'd simply been able to take the moral high ground today but who knew what she'd do tomorrow? "As attractive as the idea is, being resentful and throwing recriminations at each other won't make life easier. As you've already pointed out, we're in this together."

As soon as she finished speaking, she felt his gaze grow intent. "Did I say something wrong?" she asked, uncomfortable under his piercing stare.

He shook his head. "You said everything right. I was just thinking how lucky I am to have you," he said soberly.

His kind words, coupled with her roller-coaster emotions of the past few days, threatened to bring on tears that she couldn't explain. Intent on holding them at bay, she swallowed hard and forced a smile.

"Hold that thought for when you have to change Brody's pants again," she said lightly.

The next two weeks passed quickly and they settled into a routine of sorts, although the day came when the responsibilities of their respective jobs couldn't be ignored. On Monday, because Cole didn't report to work until eight and Sara's shift began at six, he was automatically elected to take Brody to the hospital's day care. Not that he'd minded, of course. Knowing Sara was still struggling with the situation to varying degrees depending on the day, he was doing everything possible to make life easier on her. It was the least he could do because they wouldn't be in this situation if not for him.

While he would have preferred that Sara quit her job to look after Brody, her decision to cut her hours from full-time to part-time came as a relief.

In a way, he felt guilty over Sara being the one

to disrupt her schedule and career for Brody, but she'd suggested it herself as being the logical solution. Another woman might not have been as accommodating, but he wasn't fooling himself. Her willingness to act as Brody's mother wasn't a guarantee that their marriage would return to its same open and unguarded status. He had a lot of bridges to build and instinctively he knew that if he didn't construct them properly, he and Brody could easily end up on their own.

Fortunately, as soon as he'd dropped Brody off to join the rest of the children, a toy fire truck had caught his son's eye and their parting had occurred without incident. If Cole's schedule permitted, he hoped to sneak away throughout the day so Brody could see his dad's familiar face and know he hadn't been deserted.

Now he only hoped the events he had planned for their anniversary celebration tonight would help Sara realize that she hadn't been deserted, either...

Sara's first day back at the hospital was stressful, not only because she had to add Brody to her early-morning routine but also because she'd been running at full speed ever since she'd clocked in to work. As of this morning, nearly every patient bed was filled because of a sudden influx of influenza cases. The poor respiratory-therapy staff looked frazzled as they struggled to keep pace with the demand for their services. According to the charge nurse for Sara's medical unit, the new patient she would soon receive would add to that workload.

She was on her way back to the nurses' station after silencing another IV fluid alarm when the ward clerk waved to her. "What's up, Georgia?" she asked.

"Delivery for you."

"What?"

Georgia, a forty-year-old black woman who wore a perpetual smile on her face, handed her a large mug emblazoned with the local coffeehouse logo. "This is for you."

Sara recognized the aroma wafting out of the cup and knew it was her favorite espresso flavor, skinny caramel macchiato. "Who brought this?" she asked.

Georgia shrugged. "Some kid. Didn't leave his name or ask for a tip. I asked who'd sent him and he just said you'd know."

Which meant Cole had done it. Her favorite

coffee shop had been across the street from the hospital where they'd first met and Cole would often bring espressos or lattes to share when they'd had a free minute. For him to do so now, when the nearest coffee bar was across town, showed he'd put some thought into today's surprise.

Our relationship is on indefinite probation.

As she held the still-warm cup in one hand, she understood what the drink represented. He was trying to court her again.

Suddenly, her friend Millie fell beside her. "You lucky dog," she breathed. "Where did you get that?"

"A secret admirer," Georgia supplied.

"Cole sent it," Sara explained.

"Ooh," Millie gushed in obvious envy. "Must mean you had a fantastic trip." Millie turned to Georgia. "We're taking five so she can drink that while it's still warm."

Before Sara could protest, Millie herded her to the ward kitchenette. "I've been dying to hear about your weekend for the past two weeks. Imagining the fun you two were having was the only thing that kept me going when I was at home, dealing with kids and a husband with stomach flu." She shook her head. "Why is it that none of them could come down with it at the same time? Anyway, I want to know if you did any sightseeing, or if Cole didn't let you out of your hotel room."

"We didn't go."

"Didn't go?" Millie's mouth formed a surprised O. "What happened?"

"A family emergency."

"Oh, my gosh. What happened?"

She sipped her drink, reveling in the familiar flavor. She didn't want Cole's thoughtfulness to soften her attitude toward him, but it was working quite successfully. "We became parents instead."

Millie's smile instantly spread across her face. "You're parents? Wow, Sara. I had no idea you were trying to adopt. I knew you wanted a baby for the longest time—"

As if she suddenly realized that Sara's response wasn't typical of a new mother, she cut herself off. Her smile faded and her gaze became intent. "You don't seem as excited as I would have guessed. This is a good thing, isn't it?"

"It is," she agreed obediently.

"So how old is he? What's his name? Is it a

boy or a girl? Did you get a phone call or wake up one morning and find him on your doorstep? *What?*"

Sara smiled at Millie's rapid-fire questions. "Brody James is his name and we learned about him when I got home from work on the Wednesday night before we were going to leave. The lawyer representing the mother of Cole's son broke the news to us."

Millie's eyes widened. "Whoa, back up a minute. Cole has a son?"

"Yes." She paused. "We were just as surprised as you are."

"Oh, Sara." Her expression became sympathetic. "No wonder you look stressed. He must be fairly old by now, though. You've known Cole for a long time."

"Brody is almost three."

Millie's eyes widened. "Almost three?" she echoed. "But you and Cole have been a couple for…"

Sara filled in the blank. "Six years."

Millie's eyes narrowed. "Do you mean to tell me that he *cheated* on you?"

Sara closed the door. "Could you please lower your voice?" she muttered. "I'd really rather this doesn't end up as fodder for the hospital grape-vine." The rumors would begin soon enough, especially after people saw father and son together.

"But, Sara, people can add two and two. When they do, they'll come up with four."

"Cole didn't cheat on me," she defended. "Not really. Not technically."

Her defense sounded lame to her own ears because the situation involved more than a mere technicality.

Millie looked skeptical. "Sorry, but according to my math, he had to have something going on the side if he has a two-year-old and you've been together for six."

"You may not remember, but before Cole proposed, we'd had a huge argument and we broke up. It wasn't for long, but we'd gone our separate ways. During that time, Cole met a high school friend and…Brody is the result."

"Oh, Sara." Millie's face registered distress, or perhaps it was concern, but Sara didn't bother to classify it.

"All they need to know," Sara said firmly, "is that the boy's mother was an old friend of Cole's and when she was killed, she'd granted custody to us."

"Killed?"

"Did you read about a medical helicopter crash a few weeks ago? One of the nurses on the flight was Brody's mother."

"Oh, Sara. How awful."

Millie's pitying expression was more than Sara could handle, although she knew she'd see it often in the coming days. People would speculate all they liked but, as far as she was concerned, Brody's parentage was none of their business.

"I'd appreciate it if you give the edited version to anyone who asks," she said.

Millie nodded. "Of course. But, Sara, how are you handling this? It can't be easy for you."

Not being easy was an understatement. "We're managing," she said instead. "Brody seems to have accepted Cole as his daddy and I do okay with him as long as no one refers to me in his hearing as 'mama.'"

Millie shook her head. "You're a good woman, Sara Wittman. I don't think I could be as gracious as you are under the circumstances."

"I don't always feel gracious," she admitted. "I have my days, but on the whole it's getting better." Seeing Brody's and Cole's similarities was a bittersweet reminder of so many things that had gone wrong, beginning with the secrets she'd allowed Cole to keep and ending with her failure to conceive. Some days she wanted to scream with frustration and throw things, like Brody did when life seemed to be too much to handle, but she didn't. Flying out of control would only cause Cole to suggest either a counseling visit or a prescription for an antidepressant. She didn't need or want either.

However, all things considered, as much as she wanted a baby of her own, getting pregnant right now wasn't a good idea. Bringing another child into the mix while she and Cole were sorting out their trust issues wouldn't be a wise move.

"Then why are you here at work?" Millie asked bluntly. "You should be taking maternity leave."

"I've had the past two weeks as compassionate leave," she replied. "Now I'm on part-time status for a few months. After that, we'll see how things are working out both here and at home before we decide what to do next."

Sara had been happy to accept a temporary option of part-time work because going to the hospital, even two or three days a week, allowed her to feel as if her life hadn't totally spun out of control.

A brisk knock interrupted. "Your new patient is on her way, Sara," the ward clerk announced before she disappeared again.

"Thanks, Georgia." Sara took another long swallow of her drink, savoring the taste before she set the mug in an out-of-the-way spot on the counter. "Catch you later, Mil."

Interruptions were commonplace, so she didn't worry that her friend and colleague would take offense at their abrupt parting. She reached the nurses' station in time to greet the emergency nurse who was delivering a woman in her sixties, Dorothy VanMeter, courtesy of a wheelchair.

"Caught flu?" she commiserated as she guided the pair to an empty room.

Dorothy's answer was a deep, harsh and productive cough. Sara handed her a box of tissues and set the trash can nearby for her use. When Dorothy's episode had ended, her facial color held a bluish tinge and she was holding her ribs. "I caught something," she rasped. "If this is flu, then it's something I've never had in my life. I'm so exhausted, sometimes I wonder if I can draw my next breath."

"We'll do everything we can to make you feel

better," Sara said kindly. "First, though, we'll make you comfortable so you can rest."

The next twenty minutes passed quickly as Sara listened to the nurse's update, helped Dorothy into bed and brought two blankets from the warmer to cover her. As she started her IV, Sara asked about her family.

"I have three children," Dorothy rasped. "Step-children, actually, but they don't…we aren't close."

Sara had heard similar stories before. Estrangements in families were more common than one might imagine. "Sometimes people react differently when an illness is involved," she offered. "I'll be happy to call them for you, to let them know you're in the hospital."

"Won't matter," the older woman said tiredly. "They have their own lives now." She closed her eyes and Sara took it as a signal that she either couldn't or wouldn't continue this particular conversation thread.

Fortunately, the IV fluid was dripping steadily as Cole arrived.

Her pulse jumped as it always did when she saw him looking so handsome and authoritative in his white coat, and she wondered how she could respond to him as easily as she always had. Events of the past few days should have doused the sparks quite effectively, but clearly they had not.

Sara lingered in the room while he introduced himself to Dorothy and discussed his treatment plan for her while she took mental notes. As soon as he'd finished, she washed her hands and followed him into the hallway.

"Do you really suspect whooping cough?" she asked.

"I do," he said. "According to the E.R. docs, there have been two confirmed cases in town over the weekend and her symptoms fit."

"But that's a childhood disease. We vaccinate everyone for it."

"We try," he corrected, "but the incidence has been increasing among children who haven't completed the full course and among adolescents and adults whose immunity has faded. Before you ask, though, pertussis *is* included with the tetanus booster that's recommended every ten years, but not everyone stays on top of their immunization schedules."

"I suppose not. To be honest, I'm not certain when I got my last booster shot," she confessed.

"We'd better find out," he advised, "especially with a toddler in the house."

The thought of carrying the germ home to Brody horrified her. "You're right. I'll look into it."

"Good. Meanwhile, we'll give Mrs. VanMeter supportive care and start her on an IV antibiotic. Be sure everyone uses their personal protective equipment, including a mask, when they go into her room. Hand-washing is a must, but I don't have to tell you that."

"I'll take care of it," she said, already planning to place a cart outside the room with the necessary items and post the appropriate signs on the door.

"Check with the lab. If they haven't received a sputum specimen for a *Bordetella* culture, then collect one."

"I will," she promised. "Anything else?"

"No. Er, wait, there is one more thing," he said.

While she waited expectantly, he met her gaze. "I've made plans for this evening, so don't fix dinner."

"Plans? What for?"

His dark eyes suddenly sparkled. "Tsk, tsk,

Sara. Don't tell me you've forgotten what day this is?"

"It's Monday."

"Monday. Our anniversary," he reminded her.

Her face instantly warmed. "I guess I did forget."

"Well, I didn't and so I've planned our evening."

"You planned...? But what about Brody? We can't leave him with a sitter after he's been with one all day."

"We aren't leaving him," he announced.

"Then how—?"

"I have everything under control, at least if the timing works out," he said ruefully. "I would have surprised you, but I was afraid you'd throw a tuna casserole in the oven before I got home."

Clearly, he knew her well enough to know that when she was irked at him, she served tuna casserole—his least favorite meal. No doubt with today being their anniversary, he'd been afraid she'd make him pay for their lost weekend.

"It's your lucky day," she said lightly, "because I'm out of canned tuna. I had hamburger in mind."

"Tonight calls for something a bit more special than ground beef, don't you think?"

She really didn't feel like celebrating, anniversary or not. Physical exhaustion after working a full day aside, she was still struggling to keep her emotions in check. It was ironic to realize she'd been worried at one time that he'd forget their anniversary date and yet she was the one who'd forgotten. More than likely, she'd blocked it out of her mind, she thought wryly.

"Why are you going to this much effort?" she asked bluntly. "It isn't as if you have to worry I'll send Brody back, like a refused package."

"This is about us, not Brody," he said. "You put me on probation, remember? I planned this because I know how much our anniversary weekends mean to you. Although what I arranged doesn't compare to the trip we would have taken, the occasion deserves to be marked, don't you think?"

"Oh." For the past few weeks their entire lives had revolved around one small boy to the exclusion of all else, but apparently Cole had taken time to look at the calendar. "I don't know what to say."

"Then it's a date?"

Why not? she asked herself. A quiet evening wouldn't make her feel less lacking as his wife, but it might give her an opportunity to finally establish why Cole hadn't ever been able to share his deepest secrets with her. Maybe their anniversary wasn't the best night for a soul-baring conversation, but emotionally, she hadn't been up to tackling that touchy subject before now. The shock had finally worn off and they were trying to give their relationship a solid footing again, so dinner might be the perfect opportunity to ask those hard questions.

She nodded slowly. "Yeah. Dinner sounds nice. But I don't see how—"

"Leave the details to me," he said with a smile. "Just feed Brody like usual."

"Okay. By the way, thanks for the espresso. It was really good, at least what I drank of it."

His smile lit up his face. "I'm glad."

"It must have cost you a fortune to have it delivered."

He shrugged. "Worth every penny." Immediately, he leaned down and kissed her before he strode away.

For a moment, she simply stared at his retreating back, still feeling the impression of his lips against hers. For the first time in weeks, she actually found herself anticipating an evening alone with her husband.

Brody had been eager to leave the day-care facility and his little face had brightened as soon as he saw her—which had made Sara hope she'd turned the corner and he no longer thought of her as "the lady who wasn't his mother no matter what everyone called her"—but as soon as they were back at home, he alternated between throwing his toys and yelling "No" to whatever she suggested.

Frustration became the emotion of the day but that faded to sympathy when she saw him crawl onto the sofa, scrunch the sheer curtain in his hand and peer out the window, clearly watching for someone. Occasionally, she'd hear him babble, but one word was always recognizable. Mama.

He was waiting for someone who would never come.

She'd studied enough grief counseling to know that Brody was caught between the denial and anger stages of loss. She recognized the signs and could certainly relate.

Oddly enough, though, she'd assumed she'd dealt with the psychological issues of losing their baby, but Brody's presence seemed to prove otherwise. Her grief wasn't far beneath the surface and it reared its head more often than she'd like.

However, while she couldn't sit at the window and wait for her baby to return, analyzing every abdominal ache and pain each month and hoping she'd miss her period was very similar to his faithful action of standing lookout for his mother. Like Brody, each day of unrealized hopes only made her feel the loss again and again.

In essence, they were both waiting for a miracle. Sadly, Brody didn't have a chance at getting his, but she did, provided that she and Cole repaired their trust issues. The possibility was the only thing that kept her going.

CHAPTER FIVE

BEING late had definitely tightened Cole's schedule for the evening considerably, but as he walked into the kitchen and saw his son with macaroni and cheese woven through his hair and ground into his clothes, those concerns faded.

"Brody!" he exclaimed with a hearty chuckle. "Are you eating dinner or wearing it?"

"What he isn't wearing, I am," Sara muttered.

"Daddy," Brody yelled as he held out his arms and offered a gamin smile.

Cole tickled a spot under Brody's chin as he leaned over to kiss Sara's cheek. Her stiffness bothered him, but she clearly wasn't in a loving mood, considering how frazzled she looked and how he was an hour late. He hoped she'd feel a little more charitable as the night wore on.

"So I see," he said. "Mmm, cheese."

"Among other things," she said darkly.

He pulled a strand of macaroni out of Sara's

hair. "Does this mean he hated your cooking or loved it?"

"Who knows?" She reached for the wet wash-rag and began scrubbing Brody's face and hands. "Okay, bud. Dinner is officially over."

Brody ran off to the living room and a few minutes later Cole heard the distinctive sound of toys being thrown against the wall.

Cole moved to the doorway to check on the youngster, aware that Sara had followed him. No blood and nothing broken was a good state of affairs.

Sara sighed. "I'm not sure if watching his anger is better than having him stand on the sofa and stare out the window looking for Ruth."

Cole watched Brody grab a plastic car and begin driving it in circles. He hated the thought of the little boy struggling to understand how and why his life had changed so drastically because he'd *been* that child at one time in his life, too. Granted, he'd been older—eight—but age didn't insulate one from grief and loss.

"I did the same thing," he murmured.

"Throw things or stare out the window?"

"Both. How did he handle day care?"

"According to the staff, he definitely wasn't a model child."

"Oh?"

"He had a hard time sharing the toys and got into a couple of tugging matches. Eloise had said he's such a happy-go-lucky fellow so I'm hoping he's simply expressing his frustration rather than revealing his true personality."

"He's feeling insecure and will settle down when he realizes this is his new life."

"Let's hope so," she answered fervently. "How long did it take you to adjust?"

"A while," he answered. "For me, it wasn't so much acceptance as tolerance. Then again, my situation was different."

"How so?" she asked.

He brushed aside her question. "It's too long to explain now. We have an anniversary to celebrate."

She pointedly glanced at his hands. "Celebrate with what? I didn't cook and it's obvious you didn't bring dinner."

"Nope," he said cheerfully. "I thought you deserved something more classy than food in a take-out bag."

"Ah," she said in a knowing voice. "You're

having something delivered, I assume. What kind of pizza did you order this time?"

He wasn't surprised by her guess. "It's better than pizza."

"Better than pizza?" Another crash sounded in the other room and she visibly winced. "I can't imagine."

"Pizza isn't special enough for our anniversary," he insisted.

She slowly shook her head. "Whatever it is, we should save your plans for another day. The kitchen is a mess. Brody needs his bath, I'm bushed and—"

"And I have our evening all arranged," he informed her. "I'll take care of Brody and get him ready for bed while you work your magic in here." He motioned around the room. "And when everything is spick-and-span, like it always is, I want you to enjoy a nice long, relaxing soak."

"In the tub?"

He grinned. "Where else?"

Longing flared in her eyes. "I shouldn't. We have stories to read and—"

"You can have the honors tomorrow night," he said. "Tonight, I'm letting you off the hook so you can pamper yourself. I only have two requests, though."

"Only two?"

He nodded. "Wear your little black dress and no matter what you might hear in the rest of the house, don't leave the bedroom until I call you."

Her smile slowly spread. "Sounds interesting. Okay, I'll stay put, but if you find me asleep in the tub, don't be surprised."

"If I do, I'll wake you," he promised.

Brody's bath became a challenging endeavor, but Cole learned that his son responded quite well to the authority in his deep voice. Soon Brody was wearing his pajamas and ready for his bed-time story, which Cole happily supplied. By the time Cole turned the last page, the little boy's eyelids were drooping. Clearly he'd worn himself out from his stressful day.

Although timing was of the essence this eve-ning, he allowed himself a few minutes to simply hold his son and enjoy the feeling of closeness and trust between them. He'd never experienced this depth of emotion before and it filled him with awe.

The idea of potentially losing this precious little

boy pierced his chest with an intensity so powerful he could hardly breathe.

This, he realized, was what Sara had felt after her miscarriage.

She'd lost a future little person she could love, cherish and raise to adulthood.

Intellectually, he'd understood that the child within her was gone. Without close family ties, without the experience of seeing baby brothers and sisters, nieces and nephews, he'd treated the incident as a minor event in the grand scheme of life and moved on.

However, holding Brody in his lap with his head resting against his chest, he finally realized the full depth of their loss. *Their* son would never sit on his lap, listen to a story or drool on his shoulder. It was *their* loss, not just Sara's.

While he'd known Brody would be a difficult reminder, this moment was the first time he actually felt the same pain. He truly *hadn't* known what he was asking of her and now he could only hope that Brody's presence would eventually soften the blow.

Carefully, Cole placed him in his bed, then tiptoed from the nursery. From the delicious smells coming from the kitchen, his catering company had obviously come in through the garage door Cole had left open and made themselves at home.

He found two of the Chefs-to-Go catering staff hard at work. The owner, a woman in her mid-forties, was busy with the food while her assistant was in charge of creating the ambience. After receiving last-minute instructions from both, he went to the master bedroom.

"No peeking into the other room while I take a quick shower," he ordered as he watched her put on the finishing touches to her makeup.

"You know the suspense is killing me." Her good-natured complaint sounded so much like the old Sara—the one before Brody had arrived—that he felt as if he'd stepped back in time.

"Suffer through a few more minutes," he told her. "I promise I won't be long."

He wasn't. He showered, shaved and put on the tux he'd dug out of a dusty garment bag. Satisfied with his appearance, he approached Sara, looking beautiful in the black dress he'd requested her to wear. The fabric clung to her curves and made him wish they were walking *into* the bedroom instead of walking *out* of it.

"You look fantastic," he said, regretting that he couldn't show her off at a fancy restaurant, although having her to himself came with its own benefits.

She smiled. "Thanks. You clean up nicely, too, although I hadn't expected a tux."

"As I said, it's a special night." At least, he hoped the evening would be a success. "And you're wearing my favorite perfume."

She shrugged. "It goes with the dress."

He didn't follow the logic, so he chose to believe she'd fallen into the spirit of things, which was a promising sign.

He crooked his arm. "May I escort you to dinner?"

"I'd like that very much."

As he led her into the hallway, she inhaled sharply and froze in her tracks. "Something smells fabulous. What did you do, Cole Wittman?"

"I arranged for an intimate dinner," he said, guiding her through the house toward the cozy breakfast nook where the round table had been covered with a white linen tablecloth and set for two. A single red rose floated in a rose bowl beside a white tapered candle, which flickered in the subdued light. A freestanding silver ice bucket stood beside the table, the bottle of wine he'd requested chilling inside. He flicked a switch and a romantic soundtrack began playing softly.

Sara stopped short, her jaw slack from her surprise. "Oh, my," she said, sounding surprised and a little dazed.

"Have a seat." He pulled out a chair and seated her. "I chose a special menu for tonight. I hope you'll like it."

"I'm sure I will."

"Relax while I serve the first course."

Cole quickly referred to the sheet of paper left on the counter and served the tossed salad with Italian dressing.

"This is…phenomenal," she praised as she placed her linen napkin on her lap. "I'm totally impressed."

"I'm glad," he said. "But before you dig in, I have one rule about this evening."

"Which is?"

"This night is for us and us alone."

"But what if Brody—?"

"If he wakes up, we'll deal with him, but unless he does, it's just you and me—like it would have been if we'd flown to Arizona."

She blinked in surprise and, darn it, he thought he saw her eyes shimmer. "Okay," she whispered before she repeated herself with a stronger voice. "Okay."

He pulled the bottle out of the ice and deftly removed the cork with the tool lying on the table. "Would you like some?"

"Please."

After pouring two glasses, he held his aloft. "To us and many more anniversaries."

At first, she hesitated, which gave him a moment of concern, but then she smiled and chinked her glass against his. "To us," she echoed, before she took a sip.

Relieved and feeling as if he'd done something right with this dinner, he began to enjoy the meal, noting how Sara appeared to do the same.

"How was your day?" he asked.

"At the hospital, it was busy, but you already know that," she said. "I heard two peds patients were admitted with a preliminary diagnosis of whooping cough."

He nodded. "A six-month-old and an eighteen-month-old."

"From the same family?"

"The same day care."

"Then the disease is spreading."

"Afraid so," he said ruefully. "I hope we can

nip this before the town ends up in a full-blown epidemic. Did the infection control team come to your floor?"

"Right before I left. Of course, they didn't tell us anything we didn't already know, but it never hurts to be reminded. By the way, I got my new work schedule. I'm off duty until Thursday."

"How does your weekend look?" he asked.

"It's free. Why?"

"Your parents want to visit on Sunday."

"Sunday?" Her chocolate-brown eyes widened. "Did you tell them about Brody?"

"I did."

She sat back in her chair. "Oh, dear."

"We can't keep him a secret forever," he pointed out. "Unless you don't want to see your folks for the next twenty years or so, someone had to tell them they're grandparents."

She sighed. "I know, but what…what did they say?"

"After her initial shock, your mom squealed in my ear until I thought I'd go deaf," he said wryly.

"And Dad?"

"He had a few choice words, which I won't repeat, but after he got those out of his system, he sounded excited, too."

"Did they wonder why we waited to mention Brody?"

"They did, but I told them we didn't want to raise anyone's hopes until we had squared away all the legal issues." He'd been half-surprised she hadn't called them with their announcement several weeks ago, but she'd obviously needed time to accept the situation. As much as he liked his in-laws, he had been glad of the reprieve because it had allowed the two of them to settle into the situation without well-meant outside interference.

"Good idea."

"They wanted to call you right away," he added, "but I convinced them to wait until you were at home tomorrow. So be prepared."

"I will. If they're coming on Sunday, I'll plan dinner. Did they say when they were coming?"

"As excited as they sounded, I suspect they'll arrive early and stay all day," he said, "but you'll have to ask them yourself. In any case, because Sunday will be busy with family, we should pick up our Christmas tree on Saturday."

"We don't have to get a live one," she began. "An artificial might be more practical."

"We've always had a real tree. I don't want to break our tradition, do you?"

"No, but..." Her gaze grew speculative. "I didn't realize this until now, but we've always incorporated my family traditions into our holiday celebrations, never yours. What kind of tree did your family have?"

Without thinking, he gave his standard answer. "I don't remember."

She leaned back and stroked the stem of her glass. "I don't believe you. You were eight when your parents died. That's old enough to recall your Christmases. Unless, of course, you don't trust me enough to share those stories."

He couldn't believe what he was hearing. "You think *I* have trust issues?" he asked in a tone he reserved for staff members who hadn't done their jobs to his satisfaction.

She met his gaze without flinching. "Don't you?"

"Of course I don't," he snapped.

She raised an eyebrow in response. "If you didn't have trust issues, you would have come to me with your fears instead of going to Ruth."

Back to that again! He clenched his jaw, frustrated that everything circled around to those two fateful days. "I didn't *go* to Ruth. She just happened to be in the same place that I was. And for the record, any trust issues that I had I'd resolved before we got married, remember?"

"I believe you," she said softly, "but I'm only using her as the most obvious example. Whenever I've asked about your growing-up years, you've always brushed off my questions. If not for Brody showing up on our doorstep, I would never have learned that she had been a close friend."

"Is that what this is about? You want a play-by-play account of my childhood friends?" He was incredulous. "Fine. If you'd like a list, I'll go through my yearbook and give you one."

She shook her head. "You're missing the point, Cole. There's a whole side of you I've never learned about. A side that these people knew, but I don't."

"If you're accusing me of keeping more secrets from you—"

"It isn't about secrets, as such. I want to know what makes you tick."

"We've been together for six years and you still don't know?" he asked wryly.

He'd expected her to back down, but she didn't. "You've never been open about your past. Yes, you've told me the basics, but I want more than the bare minimum facts."

He knew what she wanted—for him to spill his guts and talk about his feelings—but he couldn't give it to her. "Why do you need to hear every little detail about my youth? None of it matters. Events can't be changed."

"No, but all I'm asking is for you to share some of those stories with me. Whether they were good or bad, I really don't care. I just want to hear them so I can see how they shaped the man you are."

He'd tried to block out most of those experiences because the memories had left a bad taste in his mouth. He'd done remarkably well, too. His life had become what he'd made of it. Now Sara was asking him to reminisce about the days he'd rather forget.

Damn, but he *knew* going to his reunion had been a mistake. He should have stayed home and guzzled those margaritas in the privacy of his apartment. When the twenty-year reunion invitation arrived in two years, he'd toss it in the trash, unopened, and save himself a ton of grief.

"You said tonight was about us," she reminded him. "Which, to me, translates to a date night. And like anyone on a date, the idea is to discover new things about each other. I want to learn things about my husband that I never knew."

This wasn't how he'd planned his evening. Somehow he'd lost control and they were only on the first course.

"What I'm asking won't be easy for you," she said kindly. "I suspect you never shared those things for a reason—"

"What was the point?" he asked wearily.

"But," she continued, "we can use them to help Brody adjust to his life-changing loss in a healthy manner. You don't want him to suffer through what you did."

Could she be onto something? Would baring his soul help Brody in any way? Because the idea of his son experiencing what he did turned him cold.

"He won't," Cole said fiercely. "I won't allow it."

"Can you be sure?"

"Of course I can," he snapped. "You and my aunt are as different as night and day."

"I hope so, but unless I know what she did, what happened to you, I can't avoid her same mistakes, can I?"

While he knew in his heart that Sara's loving nature would never allow her to do the things his aunt had done—even in her hurt and anger the past few weeks, she hadn't come close to his aunt's vindictiveness. However, Sara obviously had her own fears in that regard—fears that wouldn't disappear just because he'd discounted them.

"Whatever you say won't make me think less of you," she added softly.

Logically, he supposed that was right. No one knew him as well as she did, except perhaps for Ruth, and she'd only known because she'd lived in foster care and they'd compared experiences quite often. After he'd graduated, he'd started a new life for himself—a life that had come with a carefully edited past because he hadn't wanted anyone's pity or scorn.

He definitely didn't want his own wife's, so he'd avoided the risk completely.

She reached out and touched his hand. "Let's start with your Christmases. I really want to know what they were like."

Drawing a deep, resigned breath, he forced himself to remember. "The Wittman family tradition included a real tree, but after the fire, my aunt and uncle always used artificial."

"Fire? There was a fire?"

He nodded. "It was my second Christmas in

their home. Apparently no one filled the stand with water and the tree dried out, although no one knew it. I was told to light the scented candle in the living room and my older cousin, who took pride in making my life miserable, started playing with the lighter. The next thing I knew, the tree was blazing." After twenty-five years, he still hadn't forgotten the scene, or the horror he'd felt.

"I'll bet his parents were furious at him."

"No," he said calmly. "He said I did it and, of course, they believed his story, not mine. The fire chief gave us both a severe lecture on fire safety, although I think he knew from my cousin's actions and cocky attitude that I was telling the truth. Anyway, after that my aunt and uncle always used an artificial tree." They'd never let him forget the incident, either.

"And your parents?" she asked softly. "What did you do when they were alive?"

He eyed his glass with its token splash of wine, reluctant to share the few precious memories he had. He'd only allowed himself to replay them when he felt strong enough to deal with his loss, but if Sara could face her demons, then he could do no less.

"We went to a nearby tree farm to cut our own.

It was always so much fun, traipsing through the rows in search of the perfect pine. After we sawed down ours, we drank hot apple cider and ate sugar cookies my mom had baked for the occasion while we listened to Christmas carols. It was the one time of year when she added red and green sprinkles to the frosting." Amazingly enough, he hadn't recalled that detail until just now...

"Sounds like fun," she said.

"It was. I always thought a day couldn't be more perfect."

"Did you have a similar tradition with your aunt and uncle's artificial tree?"

If he hadn't sworn off alcohol two years ago, he might have refilled his glass and drained it dry. Instead, he simply rotated the glass and watched the liquid swirl around inside.

"I really can't say. I usually wasn't around when everyone decorated it."

"You weren't? Where were you?"

"At a friend's house. Or the movies. Or the library. In high school, they usually chose a Saturday when I was out of town at a swim meet."

Sara's face registered her confusion. "Why would they exclude you?"

He watched the wine swirl faster, hardly aware that he was causing it to slosh like storm-tossed seas. "My aunt insisted on creating traditions with her own kids," he said evenly, relying on the nonchalant tone he'd perfected over the years. "I wasn't part of that group."

"How awful." Her face registered dismay. "Did they go to your school events?"

"Only if one of my cousins was also involved, which wasn't often. They weren't in the same classes or didn't have the same interests I had."

"Cole, that's terrible!" she protested.

He shrugged. "It was the way things were."

She leaned across the table and placed her hand over his. "I'm sorry."

"Why?" he asked bluntly. "It wasn't your fault."

"No, but your story explains a lot. Thank you for sharing," she said softly.

A response didn't seem indicated, so he nodded. Then, eager to change the topic, especially to one on a lighter note, he eyed her empty salad plate. "Are you ready for the main course? It's stuffed chicken breast with a sun-dried tomato pesto. And be sure to save room for dessert. Red velvet cheesecake."

That had been the menu on the night he'd proposed and he'd chosen it again for tonight to make a statement. Honestly, he couldn't say why he'd remembered those details, but he had…probably because the meal had been a prelude to a future he'd wanted but had always considered out of his reach.

Her gaze flew to meet his and she blinked in obvious surprise. "You remembered," she said, clearly awed.

"It was the most important night of my life," he said simply. "How could I forget?"

Even in the dim light, he could tell her eyes grew misty. Although he knew he wouldn't redeem himself with one special meal, it obviously wasn't hurting his cause. "Sit tight. I'll be right back."

He left the table and thanks to the instructions he'd been given, he soon returned with two steaming plates of gourmet-quality food—even if his presentation didn't quite look like the photo— and a basket of garlic-Parmesan bread.

"You… I… This is more than I'd ever imagined," she managed to say. "What a wonderful surprise."

"I'm glad you think so."

She began eating. "Did you plan all this or did

you talk some poor ward clerk into organizing it for you?"

"This might come as a surprise, but I even dialed the phone number myself."

She chuckled. "Now I really am impressed."

"And you should be," he teased. "So dig in before it gets cold."

As the dinner progressed, Cole noticed how Sara's wariness of late seemed to fade. He hoped that what he'd planned next would banish it for good.

CHAPTER SIX

SARA carefully placed her silverware across her dessert plate and leaned back, feeling remarkably mellow after two glasses of wine and a melt-in-your-mouth meal. "That was wonderful," she told him.

"I'm glad you liked it."

"The wine was delicious, too." As he attempted to fill her glass again, she covered it with her hand and shook her head. "No more or I'll be snoozing under the table." Then, because she'd noticed he'd never emptied or refilled his own glass, she asked, "Aren't you going to finish yours?"

"The hospital might call me."

"You aren't on call, are you?"

"No, but I had a couple of dicey patients today. One never knows what will happen."

Her theory suddenly seemed less like conjecture and more like fact. "You don't drink alcohol of any kind anymore, do you?"

He blinked, clearly startled by her remark. "Not really, no."

"You stopped after that weekend," she guessed.

He shrugged. "It seemed the right thing to do."

Although she'd suspected she was right, having it confirmed stunned her. "You really *did* regret your actions that evening."

"I told you I did."

She warmed under his gentle rebuke. "Hearing someone say so doesn't mean as much as when he actually modifies his behavior as a result," she defended.

"Then you believe me now?"

"I think I always did," she said slowly, "but it helps knowing you weren't merely paying lip service." Then, because she didn't know what else to say, she changed the subject.

"Thanks again for the great meal and the wonderful evening," she told him. "I'll help with the dishes—"

He rose and pulled her to her feet. "Oh, but the evening isn't over yet."

"It isn't?"

"No." Using the remote control, he selected a different playlist and music suitable for slow dancing drifted out of the speakers. He pulled her against him and because she could either follow his lead or lose her footing, she fell into step.

"What are we doing?" she asked as they moved to the song's rhythm.

"Isn't it obvious?" His breath brushed against her temple. "We're dancing."

"Yes, but—"

"Shh. You're ruining the mood," he teased.

Suddenly, being in his arms seemed like the best place to be. "Can't have that," she murmured as she allowed him to draw her close enough that she could feel his heart beat.

His hand engulfed hers and being in his embrace gave her the sense of being both protected and cherished.

For several minutes, she didn't say a word. After the stress of the last few days, it was far too easy to pretend that someone had turned back the clock and everything was as wonderful as it once had been.

"Now I know how Cinderella felt," she mused aloud.

"How so?"

"At the moment, everything is perfect, but at midnight everything changes. The coach and six white horses will become a pumpkin and a few mice. Her gown disappears into rags and—"

"And the prince eventually finds her because of the glass slipper," he said. "Did you ever wonder why her shoe didn't disappear, like everything else?"

She looked up at him. "Honestly? No. Have you?"

"Oddly enough, I have, because it didn't make sense."

Spoken like a man who looked for logic in everything. "Of course not. It's a fairy tale. You have, though, so what did you decide?"

"Well," he began slowly, "other than the author took liberties with the plot to create a happy ending, I like to think it meant that those two created enough magic during their time together that it *couldn't* disappear completely, even after they were separated at midnight. Granted, the magic was only strong enough to affect her shoes, but that small amount was able to bring them back together again."

She'd never thought of the story in those terms before and the parallel to her present circumstances didn't escape her notice. "Since when did you become a philosopher and literary critic?"

"Hey, you're the one who mentioned Cinderella."

She had. She simply hadn't expected him to draw this lesson out of it.

"It's these magical moments that make life bearable when troubles come," he continued. "They give us something to hold on to—they bring hope for happier times. That's why we have to enjoy them when they come along."

She thought of his stories about his childhood and suddenly understood her husband a little better. Granted, he'd only shared a minuscule amount, but it was a very good start.

His determination to steer clear of his few remaining family members had never made sense until now. While he'd only shared one small Christmas experience, if his aunt could treat him so poorly during the most generous, happy season of the year, what must she have done throughout the other eleven months?

Was it any wonder why he was worried about how she'd accept Brody into their lives? He'd clearly wanted to include Brody in their family, but he obviously didn't want his son to endure the constant rejection he'd had. Given his stories, she certainly couldn't blame him.

She imagined a younger Cole trying to please his aunt in order to win her approval and her love, and getting rebuffed time and again. It nearly broke her heart to imagine his disappointment and hurt until he'd finally walled off any and all expectations. At one time, he'd used the word "tolerance" instead of "acceptance" when he'd mentioned his only relatives and she understood why.

She also understood why he'd been so introspective after the lion incident. "Are you afraid of following in your aunt and uncle's footsteps? Of perpetuating their mistakes?"

"Would you blame me if I were?" he asked instead.

"No, but I don't think you have anything to worry about. You've always shown a remarkable amount of patience with Brody—far more than it sounds as if you'd received."

"I appreciate the vote of confidence."

She smiled. "You're welcome."

A distinctive wail interrupted the moment.

Sara bit back her sigh. "Our midnight has arrived," she murmured, more to herself than to Cole.

"Sooner than I'd thought, too." His voice held the same disappointed note that hers did.

"I'd better check on him," she said, but Cole didn't let go.

"I want to have more nights like this, Sara."

Considering how she'd learned a lot about her husband, it had been quite productive, not to mention thought-provoking. She'd been so certain they'd been ready to have a baby, but now she wasn't so sure. In fact, in light of Cole's personal issues, she wondered if they were truly ready to be Brody's parents, but if not for Brody's untimely arrival, she'd still be operating under her old assumptions that everything was fine. All things happened for a reason, she supposed, and helping Cole deal with his past was clearly long overdue.

Regardless, thanks to the magical evening, she felt less like she was lacking and more like a woman who could conquer any challenge, including the ones facing her.

"Yes," she said. "I'd like that, too."

Cole had just finished making his rounds on Sara's floor when he saw her approach the nurses' station. He tapped his patient notes into the computer as she sat beside him and began entering her own information.

"How's it going today?" he asked.

"Busy, as usual. Any change to Mr. Harvey's orders?"

George Harvey was a spry fellow in his seventies who'd just had a hip replaced and now seemed to be suffering an infection in the joint.

"Not really. Continue the gentamicin and send an order to the lab for an ASAP creatinine level. And page me if the results are abnormal," he said.

"Will do."

"One more thing." He logged off the computer, aware that she'd paused to listen. "Do you mind if we buy our tree tonight instead of this weekend?"

"Tonight? It'll be dark."

"So? The tree lot has lights."

"You can't wait until Saturday?"

He shrugged and grinned. "No."

"I don't know, Cole. I hate to take Brody out when it's so cold."

"It won't be any warmer this weekend," he told her. "Besides, we're painting his room, remember? That'll take most of the day by itself."

After weeks of waiting, his son's furniture had finally arrived yesterday and they'd spent all evening organizing his belongings, trying to create a space similar to that the boy had enjoyed in his old home. Thanks to the pictures Eloise had emailed, they had been fairly successful, but until they painted the walls sky blue and included the same woodland-creature wallpaper, they wouldn't achieve the result they wanted—to make Brody feel as if he were at home.

To that end, Sara had spent last night poring over the sample books from several home-decorating stores and they'd planned to begin the room's transformation bright and early on Saturday. With any luck, they'd finish before Sara's parents arrived and if not, he was sure they'd welcome the opportunity to help.

"I'd almost forgotten. Weekends just don't seem to be long enough, do they?" she said wryly.

They didn't, and this particular weekend would seem even shorter to her if she knew of the plans Cole had tucked away in his proverbial lab coat. Sally Thompson, their neighbor, had agreed to slip over on Friday evening after Brody had gone to bed so he could take Sara on another date. Granted, it would be a short night out, two hours, max, and he still didn't know for certain what they'd do—Christmas shop, perhaps?—but it would be two hours spent together, without any interruptions.

With any luck, they'd come home and spend the rest of the night setting the sheets on fire. The nights of loving each other hadn't yet resumed, but she'd stopped staring at him with those sad puppy-dog eyes and seemed more like the old Sara. Their anniversary had been a turning point of sorts and while their relationship wasn't completely back to normal, it had settled into an even—and amicable—keel.

His coffee deliveries on the days she worked hadn't hurt either.

"Two days go fast," he said. "And speaking of going fast, the day's half-over. Would you care to join me for lunch?"

His hopeful note reminded her that they hadn't coordinated their meal breaks since Brody had arrived. Granted, she'd only worked two shifts since then, but she'd purposely been too busy to join him.

"They're serving your favorite ham-and-cheese pockets in the cafeteria today," he added, as if trying to entice her. "If we don't go soon, there won't be any left."

Sara laughed at his warning, quite aware that even if the menu had included all the foods she disliked, being in Cole's company wasn't as difficult as it once had been. In fact, as much as she hated to admit it, during her days at home with Brody she missed sharing that half hour with her husband.

"Okay, I'll do my best to meet you, *after* I take care of Harvey's orders. His doctor is a real stickler for promptness, you know. In fact, it wouldn't surprise me if he calls and hounds me for the results in about thirty minutes." She grinned to soften her complaint.

He winked. "What can I say? Some physicians are real bears to work with."

"They are. Now go…" she gave him a gentle nudge "…so I can tend to my patient."

Sara hefted Brody on her hip as she followed Cole around what once had been an empty lot but was now filled with every size, shape and color of Christmas tree. Lights were strung along the perimeter and throughout the enclosure to add a festive touch. The scent of freshly cut pine was strong and intermingled with the wood smoke from the bonfire in the center. Several tall patio heaters were strategically located so that shoppers didn't feel the cold while they selected their perfect holiday decoration.

In fact, it was warm enough that Sara struggled to keep Brody's stocking cap on his head.

"Aren't the lights pretty?" she asked him, pointing overhead.

He clapped his hands and grinned.

"Which tree do you like?" Cole asked her, standing between two blue spruce that dwarfed his six-foot frame. "The skinnier or the wider?"

"How about something smaller?" she suggested. "I don't think either of yours will fit in our living room. What about those over there?" She pointed to a grouping on the left.

"Too small," Cole said. "Those are barely three feet tall."

"Too 'mall," Brody echoed. "Down."

He squirmed to the point Sara would drop him if she didn't let go, so she lowered him to the ground and he raced over to Cole. "Up," he demanded.

"You're supposed to let Sara hold you," he scolded lightly.

Brody shook his head as he clung to Cole like a leech. "Daddy hold me. Not 'ara."

Cole glanced at Sara and she shrugged. "Be my guest. He's starting to weigh more than I can handle."

Before long, Cole had perched Brody on his shoulders and the three of them wandered around the lot. By the time they'd found a tree they could live with—a five-foot Douglas fir—hauled it home and set it in the garage in a bucket of water, it was nearly Brody's bedtime.

Because Brody was so keyed up from their excursion, Sara had expected a fight about his bath and she got one. Finally, he was dressed in his footed fleece pajamas and ran into the living room with his puppy book in hand.

"Daddy, read me."

"Sara will read your story."

"No. Daddy read." The little boy's lip lowered into a pout.

"Brody," Cole warned. "You know this is how we do things. Sara reads this story."

From the beginning, they'd opted for Sara to read his puppy book because Ruth had always read it. The hope had been for him to subconsciously associate Sara with the things his mother had done, but after nearly a month it didn't seem as if they were making progress. Brody simply wasn't ready for Sara to take over the more precious routines in his memory. Tonight Sara was too exhausted to fight him.

"Read the story, Cole," she said, resigned. "He needs to go to bed."

"But—"

"Please, Cole. His bedtime should be a pleasant experience rather than a traumatic one and if listening to you will do the trick tonight, that's the price we'll pay."

He frowned and before he could protest again she sank onto her easy chair and opened the newspaper to signal an end to the discussion.

"Daddy!" came an insistent voice.

"Okay, but kiss Sara good-night," he instructed.

Obediently, Brody rushed over to her, bussed her on the cheek with an openmouthed kiss, then latched on to Cole's side.

"Only one story tonight, peewee," Cole said as he headed down the hall. "Then it's lights-out."

Sara lowered the newspaper and closed her eyes as she touched her face where Brody's sloppy kiss lingered. To Brody, this small nighttime ritual was probably a necessary evil, but to her, it was another bittersweet moment among many. If not for her miscarriage, she might have been feeling *her* child kiss her good-night, not because he'd been coaxed but because he loved her as his mother.

The rumble of her husband's deep voice and Brody's childish giggles carried down the hall. Wanting to be a part of their circle, even if only from the sidelines, she tiptoed to the bedroom door and watched.

Cole was sitting on the padded rocking chair with Brody on his lap as the two gazed intently at the colorful pages of his picture book. Her husband changed the tone of his voice to match the characters, which clearly tickled his son's funny bone. Occasionally, Cole would glance at his son and hug him. Brody smiled, clearly feeling secure in his father's love.

At one time, Cole had claimed he needed her help to be Brody's father, but ever since that day at the store and the incident with Larry the lion, as far as she could tell, he was doing just fine on his own. As for Brody, the little boy seemed to thrive under his dad's attention, which only confirmed that, regardless of how difficult her decision had been, she'd made the right one for the two of them.

The ironic thing was that Cole had been afraid of being an inadequate father, but she was the one who felt completely inadequate for the task of raising *this* child. No matter what she did, Brody still hadn't warmed to her and she wondered if he had sensed her reservations about bringing him home from the very beginning. Then again, the dynamics of her relationship with Brody were different than what she'd have with her own child. Brody had to sort through his grief and his anger over being told that Sara was taking his mother's place. While a child inherently trusted his or her parents, she had to *earn* Brody's.

Just like she was trying to earn his father's.

Their heart-to-heart conversations so far had been great. She'd learned so much about her husband that she hadn't known before. His focus on excellence had begun long before he'd entered medical school, she'd discovered, in order to gain his family's approval. When he'd accepted that they were ambivalent about his achievements, he'd worked even harder because of the personal satisfaction. In some respects, she felt as if they'd done things backward by sharing these things after they'd married rather than before, but, regardless of the timing, she wanted to believe the seeds of trust were beginning to take root, in both of them.

If they were getting to know each other all over again, wasn't it time she stopped keeping him at arm's length? She'd declared their relationship on probation while waiting to reach a nebulous milestone, but wasn't she, in essence, acting like his aunt, who'd withheld her love and affection as a way to control him?

It seemed ironic that Brody's presence had caused the cracks in their armor to finally be revealed. It would be even more ironic if Brody helped to repair them.

Cole left Brody's room and went in search of his wife. Although he was more than happy to read Brody his bedtime stories, he refused to do so at Sara's expense. The boy would never learn to depend on her if they catered to his every whim.

He found her in the kitchen. "We need to talk," he began firmly.

Sara turned away from the stove and handed him a mug. "I already know what you're going to say."

"You do?" He eyed the steaming cup in his hand and inhaled the spicy apple fragrance. "What's this?"

"Hot cider. If it wouldn't be so late, I'd whip up a batch of sugar cookies so we could continue your Christmas tree tradition, but I had to create a plan B. We're having the cider now and I'll have the cookies ready for when we decorate on Saturday."

He wouldn't have been more surprised if she'd handed him an early Christmas present. Then again, perhaps she had…

"I can't believe you went to the trouble," he said.

"It's no trouble." She blew across the top of her drink in an obvious effort to cool it to a drinkable temperature. "Correction. It will be when I'm trying to make cookies tomorrow with Brody trying to help, but there's another generation of Wittmans, so it's time we reestablish the Wittman family traditions, don't you think?"

He stared at her, taking in her tousled hair, her gentle smile and the soft expression in her eyes. After working all day, coming home to prepare dinner and then going on a shopping excursion, she was the most beautiful thing he could possibly hope to see.

Hope that she'd finally forgiven him flared. He wanted to believe she had but didn't dare in case he was mistaken.

Maybe he was dreaming. The hot mug in his hand indicated otherwise.

"Yeah," he said, speechless. "Thank you."

"So let this be a lesson to you for next year," she scolded without heat. "We have to plan our tree purchase in advance so I'm not caught unprepared, like I am now."

She was talking about *next Christmas.*

"Then you're planning to stick around?" he asked, wanting confirmation.

For a second, she seemed taken aback by his question. Then her expression became speculative as if she realized she'd spoken of the future in a general way rather than with any real plans. "Did you think I wouldn't?"

He shrugged. "Your suitcase is still packed."

"My suitcase?" She sounded as puzzled as she looked, but in the next instant her expression became sheepish. "It is, isn't it? I hadn't realized…"

He didn't see how she could overlook that detail. He saw the bulging piece of luggage every time he walked in and out of their bedroom. Having lived his entire life with an escape plan in place, he recognized it for what it was. Oddly enough, now he understood how the concept had troubled Sara because it bothered him to see her do the same.

"I'll take care of it," she said.

He pressed on. "I've also seen the way you sometimes look at Brody."

"Oh? And what way is that?"

"Like you're sad and ready to cry. He reminds me of the baby we lost, too."

She stared at him, incredulous. "He does? You've never said."

"I should have," he said. "I should say a lot of things, but I don't."

"Because you don't want anyone to discover your weak spots."

He'd never considered his reticence in those terms. He'd learned to hold his feelings and thoughts close to his chest because some things were just too personal to share while others—his mind froze as he suddenly realized how accurate she was—made him vulnerable. If there was one thing he'd learned, it was to avoid being vulnerable.

But if he couldn't be open and honest with his wife, then who *could* he be open and honest with?

He nodded, surprised by her perception. "When I think about losing the baby," he began slowly, "*our* baby, it hurts."

"Really? You never acted as if you cared."

He thought back to those days and realized she was partially correct. "I didn't have time to get used to the idea before he…was gone."

"I really didn't either," she admitted. "And that almost makes losing him worse. Maybe if I'd suspected sooner, I would have done something different. I'd have skipped my aerobics class or wouldn't have helped lift a patient—"

"No, don't go there. Don't blame yourself. It was merely nature's way."

She nodded. "Yeah. Survival of the fittest and all that." Her smile seemed weak. "Unfortunately, when you want something so badly you ache from the wanting, blaming it on Mother Nature doesn't always help. And sometimes when I'm around Brody…" Her voice died.

"It only emphasizes what we lost," he finished for her. "I discovered that, too. It wasn't just a mass of tissue or a few cells, but a little boy or girl who'd grind macaroni into his hair, suck his thumb or bring a book and say, 'Daddy, read me.'"

"Then you really do understand."

He met her surprised gaze and nodded. "Which is why I wouldn't have been shocked if you'd decided to walk away, although I hoped and prayed you wouldn't."

"The idea seemed attractive at times," she admitted, "but we promised to stick together through good *and* bad times. As I want our marriage to last and our family to grow, then—"

"After Brody's tantrum tonight, do you really want more children?" he asked, incredulous.

"I do," she said with a soft smile. "Maybe not immediately but soon. If you recall, we'd talked about having four."

He hadn't forgotten. Running after Brody kept him busy enough; he couldn't imagine keeping tabs on four at once and he said so.

She laughed. "It's a matter of organization. The important thing is that there will be four individuals who need us to look after them and guide them into adulthood."

"It's the years between babyhood and adulthood that are daunting," he said dryly. All that aside, though, the one thing he wouldn't mind would be *creating* them. It seemed like such a long time since he'd made love with his wife...

"As you brought up his tantrum," she continued, "you're going to tell me to be more firm with him, aren't you?"

He leaned against the counter and cradled his mug in his hands when he'd rather cradle the woman a few feet away. "We can't cater to his whims, not if we ever want him to accept you as his mother."

"I'm beginning to doubt if we ever will," she murmured.

"What makes you say that?"

She paused, her expression downcast. "When Brody's with you, he acts as if the sun rises and sets in his daddy while I'm merely someone to tolerate. I feel like a third wheel—handy to have around in a pinch but useless the rest of the time."

"You're imagining things."

"I'm not, Cole. You might think he's more accepting of me when you aren't around, but he isn't. Rather than follow me around the house, he sits by the door like he's waiting for Ruth to walk in at any minute. It breaks my heart to know he's hurting and I want to minimize that as much as I can, but he won't let me."

Unable and unwilling to stop himself, he set his mug on the counter and drew her into his arms. "He will. It's only been a few weeks. Of course he's hurting, but he can't avoid the truth. One day, he'll wake up and the hole in his chest won't feel quite so big because we—*you*—will be filling up the space."

Having her against him had never felt so good. He ran a finger along her jawline, marveling at her soft skin. "Just like you filled my empty spaces."

He lowered his head and brushed his mouth against hers. As her lips parted in invitation, he continued his gentle assault, uncertain of where this might lead.

"I've missed this," he murmured between his kisses. "I've missed having you next to me."

"I have, too," she answered, "but—"

"No buts," he responded as he nuzzled the spot on her neck that had always made her melt. "I want to make love with my wife. Tonight. *Now.*"

"Oh, my," she breathed. "I want it, too."

He ran his hand under her shirt. "Then what are we waiting for?"

"To finish our conversation?"

"Later," he promised. "Much later."

Eager to enjoy the comfort of his own bed, he pulled away and began flicking off the lights.

"What are you doing?" she asked.

"Being discreet. We have a two-year-old in the house."

She giggled, sounding like the girl he'd married. "I'd forgotten."

It gave him immense satisfaction to know that she had, because it meant he hadn't lost his ability to drive his rational-thinking wife into a mindless state. "I haven't."

He tugged her toward the door, but she stopped. "The stove," she reminded him.

"Oh, yeah."

After a two-second detour to turn off the burner, Sara found herself swept along to their bedroom where Cole closed the door with a quiet snick.

She stripped off her sweatshirt and stepped out of her jeans, aware of Cole doing the same, but before she could dive under the comforter, he stopped her.

"I want to see you," he said hoarsely. "Like the first time."

"The first time wasn't in the dead of winter," she returned.

His grin turned feral. "You won't be cold for long."

Under his heated gaze and reverent hands, the chill in the air no longer affected her and she reached out to conduct her own exploration.

She'd seen him naked before and knew his body almost as well as she knew her own. His shoulders were broad, his muscles defined from the hours spent on his weight bench in the basement, and the crisp dark hair on his chest that arrowed down to below his waist was soft against her skin.

"Tell me you want this as much as I do," he said.

"I want this."

"Then far be it from me to withhold Cinderella's wish." His fingers found her nipples and toyed with them until she ached.

"Oh, Cole," she whimpered, and she whimpered again when his mouth took over and his hands ventured into other territory with such skill that she found herself standing on the brink.

She gripped his shoulders and whimpered again, this time more loudly.

"Shh," he said, his voice as soft as his caress. "We can't wake Brody."

"Mmm," she murmured as his hands drove her wild.

Lost in her sensation of fireworks, she only vaguely noticed when they landed against the sheets. "Oh, don't stop. Please."

"I love it when you beg," he teased, "but don't worry. I'm not stopping. Not now, not ever."

Impatient, she tugged him onto her and welcomed him into her body. Slowly, he moved, until she thought she'd die from impatience. His hands roamed again, locating the responsive areas he'd mapped earlier. Sensation after sensation rocked her, demanding release, but she forced herself to hold back until he was ready.

Finally, just when she couldn't bear it any longer, his shudders drove her off the edge. They soared together until the tremors stopped and she slowly drifted into the most peaceful state she'd ever experienced.

Sara snuggled against Cole's back, grateful for his warmth and remarkably content for the first time in weeks. She'd missed this closeness and was glad they'd finally found their way back to each other again.

She smiled, thinking of how intense their lovemaking had been. It was as if digging into Cole's past, encouraging him to face his fears, as well as forgiving and forgetting previous mistakes, made a powerful combination.

As she lay there, she decided her first order of

business that morning would be to unpack her suitcase. For all she knew, Brody had picked up on her subconscious symbol of escape, which was why he still resisted her attempts to get close to him. With any luck, he'd sense the change in her attitude and respond accordingly.

Pleased with her decision, she slowly drifted off, but an odd sound startled her awake. She listened, but just as she dismissed it as nothing, she heard it again.

A child's whimper.

"Cole." She nudged him. "Brody's crying."

"Hmm," he mumbled, unmoving.

She touched his warm shoulder. "You have to see what's wrong."

"Okay," he murmured sleepily. "I'll go."

A subsequent soft snore indicated her request hadn't registered.

"Cole," she urged again.

"Uh-huh…going," he muttered.

When he didn't move, Sara knew she had to take matters into her own hands. After all, if she didn't sleep well tonight, she could nap tomorrow when Brody did. Cole didn't have that luxury. Still, uncertain of what she might do to console the boy, she slipped out of her warm cocoon, blindly slipped on her nightgown and fuzzy robe, then padded into Brody's room.

He wasn't there.

Panic-stricken into full wakefulness, she wondered what had happened to him. News stories of children abducted out of their beds flooded her mind. She was ready to throw on the lights and yell for Cole when she heard the whimper again.

She followed the sound and found Brody curled in a ball on the sofa, with his teddy bear and blanket. He was asleep, but the hall night-light was strong enough for her to see the wet glimmer on his cheeks.

"Oh, sweetheart," she said, sad that he was clearly acting out his dreams. "Let's go to bed."

She tried to pick him up, but he protested. "No-o-o."

"Brody, you'll sleep so much better in your own bed," she coaxed.

His eyes remained closed, but his objection was plain. "No."

Sara debated waking Cole, then decided she had to resolve this on her own. This time she picked him up and cradled his weight against her. And when he mumbled "No," she simply rocked him.

Eventually, he melted against her and she leisurely strolled back to his room where she changed his wet diaper and settled him in his bed. "Good night, sweet prince," she said as she kissed his chubby little cheek.

Minutes later, she'd just started to doze when she heard the same sound.

Once again, she found Brody on the sofa, crying softly in his sleep.

Certain they'd both spend the night traipsing back and forth, which meant no one would sleep well if at all, she pulled a spare comforter out of the linen closet and returned to the living room. Ignoring his weak protests, she tucked the blanket around them and settled down for the rest of the night with Brody cradled in her arms.

"Good night, young man," she murmured against his tear-dampened hair. "Sleep tight."

He let out a deep sigh and nestled against her, as if he'd either finally found the comfort he'd been searching for or he was too exhausted to fight her. Yet, as his shuddering sobs slowly evened into peaceful breathing, she felt satisfied to have been the person who'd seen him through his nightmare.

In his half-asleep state, he probably didn't realize she'd been the one providing comfort, but she didn't mind. He might reject her nurturing while he was awake, but he obviously was content with it while he was asleep.

This certainly wasn't the way she'd envisioned motherhood would be, but for now it was better than nothing.

CHAPTER SEVEN

"OH, COLE, how could you?" Sara wailed on Sunday as soon as she walked into the kitchen where he and Brody were snacking on her home-made chocolate-chip cookies.

"How could I what?" he asked, popping the last bit of evidence into his mouth.

"Eat cookies right before lunch. I was saving those for this afternoon."

"We only took two and, besides, please note." He pointed to the artfully arranged tray she'd prepared. "I moved the rest around so no one will ever notice a few are missing."

"I'm not worried about the numbers or how the platter looks," she groused. "Brody's the one with chocolate smeared from ear to ear."

He glanced at his son, who stared back at him with wide-eyed innocence as if to ask, What's wrong? As Sara had said, chocolate and cookie crumbs were all over his face and the hands clutching the cookie were grubby as well. To make matters worse, a dark smear ran across the appliqué of Rudolph on Brody's red pullover sweater.

"He'll wash."

"Yes, but my parents will be here any minute and I don't have time to change his clothes again. You were *supposed* to keep him clean while I got ready," she said sternly. "We're trying to make a good impression."

He smiled at her distress. "Your parents are going to be too excited to notice he's wearing a few crumbs and stained with chocolate. If they do, they'll understand. They had four kids of their own, remember?"

She shot him an exasperated glare. "That's not the point, Cole. I wanted everything to be perfect—"

The doorbell rang and her exasperation turned to shock. "Oh, dear. They're here." She glanced at the clock. "They're *early!*" she wailed.

For an instant he wanted to wail with her. In spite of his assurances that Sara's parents could arrive when they wished and stay as long as they liked, in spite of his easygoing manner and the smile on his face, his gut churned. He'd spent most of his childhood being on the receiving end of thinly veiled hostility and he braced himself for more of the same today. As a teen, he'd sworn he'd never allow himself to be put in the same situation, and yet here he was, about to endure it again.

The only difference was, as a kid, he hadn't deserved such treatment. Fortunately, he'd usually been able to escape to his room or a friend's house, or even his school books, but that luxury wouldn't be granted him today. Today, he *deserved* his in-laws' wrath and he'd bear it with grace because deep down he knew they were only acting out of love for their daughter.

He hoped she realized how lucky she was.

"Take a deep breath," he ordered with undisguised humor. As soon as she obeyed, he added, "Now, let your parents inside before they freeze on the front porch."

While Sara flew out of the room, Cole bent down to brush off the worst of the crumbs on his son's clothing. "Shall we meet your grandparents?" he asked.

Brody babbled something that Cole took to mean agreement.

As the sound of Greg and Marcia Adams's voices drifted in his direction, Cole hoisted Brody into his arms and held him like a talisman as he went to greet Sara's parents.

Greg was a few inches shorter than Cole, gray-haired and, thanks to his job as a mechanic and his weekend job as a woodcutter, extremely fit for a man his age. As he noticed Cole and Brody hanging in the background, his normal smile spread widely and his eyes softened.

"There's my grandson," he said, sounding like a proud grandfather. "He's a fine-looking boy, isn't he, Marcia?"

Marcia, an older version of Sara, nodded with her eyes suspiciously bright. "Oh, my, yes. I'm so glad our appointment for a family photo isn't for another two weeks. Now he'll be included. What do you think about everyone wearing red and—?"

"Enough about the annual photo," Greg chided his wife good-naturedly. "Brody and I have more serious things to discuss than what to wear. Like what's in my box of goodies."

He picked up the large box at the door and carried it to a draft-free spot in front of the Christmas tree. After a bit of coaxing, Brody joined him in the game of pulling out all sizes and shapes of brand-new cars and trucks.

Cole watched the two hard at work, pleased that his son had such a kind and forgiving grandfather. Yet how could he not? Sara was a reflection of those traits. As his gaze landed on her, he silently thanked the fates for bringing her into his life. As far as he was concerned, she was his saving grace.

Suddenly, Brody ran out of the room and returned with more toy cars in his arms.

"Goodness!" Marcia exclaimed. "I do believe he has as many vehicles to play with as you had dolls, Sara."

Cole's ears perked. "How many did you have? You never told me you had a *collection*," he teased his wife.

"Because I didn't *collect* them," she informed him grandly.

"Yes, you did," Marcia corrected her. "Maybe not in the sense of acquiring them just to look at, but somehow they always managed to come home with you." She addressed Cole. "Whenever we passed a thrift shop, we had to go in so she could see if anyone had dropped off a doll. If one was there, we had to buy it."

Cole eyed his wife, surprised to hear this story.

And yet he wasn't. "Why haven't I heard this before?"

"Because I'd forgotten myself until now," Sara answered. "For the record, though, we didn't buy *every* doll we came across."

"Maybe not, but you came close," Greg added from his spot on the floor. "I built enough miniature bunk beds that I could make them in my sleep. Thank goodness we had enough bedrooms for her and her sister to each have their own, because no one could walk around in hers."

"You made seven beds," she defended. "I only kept fifteen dolls and one always slept with me."

"Fifteen?" Cole asked.

She shrugged. "It wasn't so many, really. I took the dolls that I didn't think anyone else would buy so I could give them a home."

"You *rescued* dolls?" Cole asked.

Sara grinned. "Sure, why not? Someone had to."

"But *dolls?* Why not cats or dogs?"

"We didn't have room for pets," she said. "The expense of feeding them would have been horrific and dolls didn't have to go to the vet."

"What made you start in the first place?" Cole asked.

"I can answer that," Marcia interjected. "Sara always complained that because she was the baby of the family, no one needed her for anything. So I told her to find something she could call her own. She always loved dolls and one day—"

Sara picked up the story. "One day, I was at a friend's house and she had a doll that she didn't want anymore because its clothes were torn and her brother had cut off one pigtail. Because I knew my dad could fix anything..." she cast a benevolent glance at her father "...I brought her home and the rest, as they say, is history."

"And, boy, was she right," Greg added affectionately. "She dragged home dolls that had more problems than you can imagine. Missing eyes, hair, arms, legs, you name it. Her mother and I became good enough at repairing them that we could have opened a side business."

"Don't forget that once they were restored, I found them new homes," she pointed out.

"True," her father admitted. "She only *kept* fifteen, but I'll bet we had hundreds over the years."

Sara laughed. "Now, Dad, I'm sure you're exaggerating."

"Want to bet?" he retorted without heat. "So,

Cole, be prepared for Brody to follow in her shoes. With all these cars and trucks, you could end up adding master mechanic skills to your medical degree."

"I'll keep it in mind," Cole answered. "But, Sara, with fifteen dolls, how did you ever play with them all?"

"I had a system," she began.

"I'll say," her mother interrupted. "I can't tell you how many times we had to wait on Sara because she was feeding or changing or bathing one of them."

Clearly, Sara's mothering gene had been activated early in her life. In light of the doll story, she probably felt she was limiting herself to her dream of four. No wonder she was so impatient to start their family.

Cole listened to their good-natured banter, knowing that this was the sort of home life he wanted Brody to experience. He wanted him to feel loved enough to say and do what he wanted without fear, secure in the support of his parents.

As the stories continued, oddly enough his own insecurities inched their way to the surface. Had Sara reconciled so quickly with him because she loved him, or because he was only a means to the end she wanted?

"Our ward is taking on the overflow from Peds," Beverly McCarter announced during an impromptu early-morning ward staff meeting on Monday. Beverly was the medical-surgical unit supervisor and the strain of handling the increased patient census with a shortage of staff showed on the forty-eight-year-old's face. However, she wasn't the only nurse who sported dark circles under her eyes. To varying degrees, everyone was working overtime.

Except for Sara, of course. When she considered her lack of progress with Brody, she'd glumly thought her time would be better served if she worked more hours to take care of people who really needed her, but, as her mother had reminded her yesterday during their visit, she and Brody would never form a bond if they didn't spend time together.

"We're getting peds patients?" someone asked. As glances were exchanged, plainly most of the nurses were feeling out of their element when it came to caring for the younger set.

"Don't panic," Bev ordered. "They're only

sending us the older kids, ten and up. We decided it would be in everyone's best interests if the experienced peds nurses looked after the littlest."

"That's a relief," another nurse remarked.

"Age aside, we have six very sick kids with us now," Bev reported. "They range from age ten to fourteen and the doctors are warning we might get more."

"Do they all have whooping cough?" Sara asked.

"With complications," Bev told her. "Two have had seizures and four have secondary bacterial pneumonia. I might remind you that pneumonia is the most common cause of pertussis-related deaths, so don't take their conditions lightly. These are very sick children."

"Shouldn't they be in ICU?" Millie asked.

"ICU is also bursting at the seams," Bev said wearily. "Once again, I want to remind everyone that transmission of this disease is through direct contact with respiratory secretions. I don't want to see anyone without proper protective equipment, including a mask. Granted, once these kids have finished their five-day erythromycin regime, they aren't considered contagious, but in the meantime they are."

"So who's the doctor in charge?" another nurse asked. "Do we call Dr. Wittman, or one of the pediatricians?"

"Dr. Wittman is our first contact as usual, but he's working closely with the pediatricians and the family physicians. Unless he tells you otherwise, run everything you see, do or suspect by him. Any questions?"

The group dispersed with each outgoing nurse giving specifics about her patients to those who were relieving them. In addition to her other patients, Sara had been assigned siblings Mica and Mandy Berton, who had pneumonia.

Normally, pertussis patients were isolated but because these two came from the same household, they were allowed to share one of the larger rooms so their mother could stay with them.

After donning her protective gear, including a mask, Sara found the woman dozing in a recliner between the two beds. Knowing how exhausted she must be, Sara quietly began to replace Mica's bag of IV fluid.

Mrs. Berton stirred. "Is it morning already?" she murmured.

"Afraid so. Feel free to go back to sleep. I'm only going to check their vitals. After the night they had, I suspect they won't even know I'm here."

"They both had a rough time," Mrs. Berton admitted. "If one wasn't coughing, the other was. In between that, the respiratory therapist was here giving breathing treatments. I was beginning to think we were at a bus stop from all the people coming and going."

Sara smiled as she noted blood pressures and pulse rates. "It seems that way at times, doesn't it?"

As she finished her tasks, their mother asked, "How are they?"

Sara wasn't inclined to speak as bluntly as the night nurse had to her. *No real improvement. Persistent mild fever with intermittent spikes. Coughing spells often result in cyanosis.*

"From what the night staff told me," she said instead, "no real change."

Mrs. Berton's sigh said it all. "I'd hoped we'd see some improvement by now."

Sara would have liked that, too.

"How much longer can they go like this?"

Another question Sara couldn't—and wouldn't—

answer. "I wish I could give you an exact time-table, but so much depends on staying ahead of any secondary problems."

"Like their pneumonia."

"Like the pneumonia," Sara agreed. "We're doing everything we can to help them kick this. Unfortunately, recovery takes time."

Mrs. Berton nodded, but the bleakness in her eyes said that she wasn't particularly comforted by Sara's remark.

"I know this is rough on you," Sara added, "but sometimes a little thing like a break to run home and shower can change our perspective. Maybe you'd like to do that when the RT comes in?"

According to the nursing reports, the children's mother hadn't left the hospital since they'd arrived two days ago.

"My husband is coming in after he takes our youngest boy to school. Until then, I have to stay. I *need* to stay." She gave a mirthless chuckle. "It sounds crazy, but I feel like as long as I'm here, they're going to be all right."

Sara understood what she meant. "A lot of parents have told me that," she said kindly.

"Mica always drove me crazy when he asked, 'What's to eat, Mom?' before I'd cleaned the kitchen from the last meal. Now it would be music to my ears." She glanced at Sara. "I won't ever complain again about that boy's bottomless stomach."

"When he's past the worst of this, he'll be hungry again. You'll see."

Mrs. Berton sighed. "I hope so. I'd be devastated if the worst happened…"

"Of course you would be," Sara murmured. "But, as I said earlier, they're holding their own." Her pager went off and she checked the display. Today would definitely be one of those days that would go down in the annals of nursing infamy… "I have to go, but I'll be back as soon as I can. Meanwhile, you know where the call button is. Let me know if you sense a change of any kind."

Sara checked in another new patient—thankfully, this one was a thirty-year-old woman with a complicated leg fracture as a result of a car accident rather than another whooping-cough case—before continuing on her rounds. Then she had to make a quick trip to the blood bank to pick up a unit of blood for a severely anemic patient. On the way back, she stepped into the elevator to find Dr. Eller, her ob-gyn.

"Congratulations," the fifty-four-year-old specialist told her with a smile. "Cole told me your good news. You're looking well for being a new mother."

She smiled, tamping down the lingering disappointment that motherhood hadn't come in the manner she'd expected. While all of her energies were focused on Brody, she still had unanswered questions about her own health—questions that she hoped Dr. Eller could answer in order to ease her mind.

"Thanks," she answered politely. Then, because the elevator was empty and there was no time like the present, she pressed on. "I'd like to set up an appointment to see you, though."

"Feeling tired, eh?" He grinned. "I haven't met a woman yet who has a two-year-old and isn't tired."

"This isn't about feeling tired or stressed," she corrected him carefully, hating to go into detail in an elevator, even if they were the only people on board. "While now probably isn't the best time for me to get pregnant, I'd like a reassurance that when we *are* ready, I *can* have a baby."

His bushy eyebrows drew together. "You miscarried about, what, six months ago?"

"Nine," she corrected.

Dr. Eller stared thoughtfully at her before he spoke. "How long has it been since you had a thorough physical?"

She shrugged. "I have no idea."

He nodded. "Then we'll start with that, just to rule out any of the obvious health issues."

"Perfect," she said, relieved he was willing to be proactive.

His gaze grew intent. "I talked to Cole the other day and he didn't mention you were concerned."

Not long ago, she *had* been concerned because not having a child made her feel as if an important part of her was missing. Brody's presence had helped, but while she could accept him as part of their family, Cole's son didn't fulfill her personal dream of having a baby of her own. Granted, getting pregnant had dropped its top-priority status in relation to the other events in her life but, regardless of those events, she still had questions that demanded answers.

"I'm more curious than concerned," she explained.

He smiled. "Understandable. In any case, a physical is always the best place to begin. Call my office for an appointment and meanwhile I'll have my nurse phone in lab orders."

Her knees shook with relief. "Thank you."

"After I see those results—it may take a week or so to get them—we'll talk. How does that sound?"

"Marvelous. You don't know what this means to me, Dr. Eller."

The door slid open and he stepped out. "I haven't done anything yet," he said cheerfully, before he disappeared around the corner.

Sara leaned weakly against the rail as the door closed. Perhaps she should have talked this over with Cole before she talked to Josh, but when the opportunity had presented itself, she'd seized it. Cole surely couldn't fault her for that, could he?

However, the answer to that question never came because as soon as she arrived at her floor, she immediately started her patient's blood transfusion. By the time she returned to the Bertons' room, where the respiratory therapy technician was finishing up the children's treatments, nearly an hour had passed.

"What do you think?" she asked the woman after she followed her into the hall.

"To be honest, I'd expected them to be better by now. Has Dr. Wittman come by to see them this morning?"

"Not yet."

"See if he can come sooner rather than later," the therapist advised. "Mica's lung function seems to be dropping. I don't know if a different antibiotic might be helpful, but see what he thinks. Page me if he wants me to come more often."

"Will do."

She returned to find Mica coughing and clutching his abdomen. "Hurts," he murmured.

"What's wrong now?" his mother asked, obviously worried.

"It could be something as simple as sore muscles." Sara frowned. "But I'll be sure to point it out to the doctor." She punched in a text message to Cole's phone. "He's running later than usual, but don't worry. He'll stop by soon, I'm sure."

Sara returned to her station to record her nursing notes. Then, hearing an alarm which seemed to originate in the Berton children's room, she gowned again and went inside.

This time, the children's father was in the room, talking in a loud whisper to his wife. A big, burly man wearing jeans and a plaid flannel shirt under the paper hospital gown, he was the sort one didn't want to meet in a dark alley. The glare he shot her above his mask when she walked into the room only reinforced her opinion.

"Tom," his wife said, "this is Sara, and she's their nurse today."

"I don't care who she is," he retorted hotly. "I want to talk to the doctor."

Sara identified the source of the alarm—kinked tubing—and silenced the offending noise, using those few seconds' delay to modulate her tone in the face of the man's hostility.

"And you will," Sara promised once the only noise in the room was the whoosh of the humidifier. "I've paged Dr. Wittman and he should be arriving shortly. He's always happy to talk to family members."

"My kids aren't getting better."

"We're doing everything we can—"

"It isn't enough," the man insisted. "They should be in ICU or have constant nursing care or something."

"We're giving fluids and antibiotics, and the breathing treatments are delivering medicine into their lungs," she explained. "We simply have to wait for our measures to get ahead of the infection."

He approached her, his face grim. "That's the best you got? To tell me that we have to *wait?*"

"Tom," his wife chided. "Yelling at the nurse won't help. She's—"

"You aren't hearing me," he growled at Sara, ignoring his wife's plea. "My kids are not getting better." With each carefully enunciated word he poked a finger into her shoulder hard enough to throw her off balance.

Sara had dealt with belligerent patients before but this guy had caught her off guard. The call button seemed a million miles away, but even if she reached it, she had no guarantee that anyone would answer it soon enough to help her defuse the situation.

"And I want to know what you're going to do about it," he continued grimly.

"I know you're concerned and upset," Sara said evenly in spite of her racing heart, "but getting angry won't help them or you."

"Tom," his wife urged again. "Calm down."

"I will *not* calm down," he rasped. "I want to know why my kids aren't getting better and what you so-called medical *experts* are doing about it."

This time, as he reached out to poke her again,

Sara found herself being unceremoniously moved out of the way.

"I will tell you *exactly* what we're doing, Mr. Berton." Cole's eyes glittered with fury. "*We're* all going to take a deep breath while *you* put your hands in your pockets. And if I see you touching my wife or any of the staff again, *for any reason,* I will ask Security to escort you from the building. Do I make myself clear?"

Although he spoke pleasantly, Sara heard the steel in his voice. Obviously Tom did, too, because he shuffled back a few steps.

"Didn't mean to push her," he mumbled as he avoided Sara's eyes. "I was just trying to get some answers."

"Answers come easier when the questions are asked in a civil tone and the help isn't threatened," Cole answered coldly. "Can we continue this conversation like adults or not?"

As Tom focused on a point near the ceiling, his eyes suspiciously as red as his wife's, Sara took pity on them. "No harm done," she said softly. "Tom was just concerned about his kids."

While Tom nodded, his eyes expressing his gratitude, Cole frowned. He shot her a glance that promised the discussion was merely postponed and not over, but she simply smiled at him.

"Tom, why don't you and your wife step outside while Dr. Wittman examines Mica and Mandy?" she suggested. "The waiting room at the end of the hall has a pot of coffee. Have a cup and when we're finished, we'll find you."

Mrs. Berton nodded. "I think that's a wonderful idea. Tom, shall we go and let the doctor work?"

Tom hesitated, as if he was uncertain about leaving, but between Sara's encouraging smile and his wife tugging on his arm, he strode from the room.

"What in the world were you doing?" Cole muttered. "Why didn't you—?"

"Cole, please. Not now. We have two sick kids and two worried parents." She immediately went into nurse mode, repeating everything the respiratory therapy technician had reported, as well as adding her own observations.

He examined Mica first. "Do we have his sputum culture results?"

"They were posted an hour ago," she replied, pulling up the document on the computer screen.

He studied the report. "According to this, the drug we're using is only marginally effective, so

I'm going to switch to a higher-powered antibiotic. Continue with everything else."

After noting his orders in the computer, she joined him at Mandy's bedside.

"Hi, hon," Cole said softly. "How're you doing today?"

"Not…not so good."

"I'm not surprised," he said. "But you'll be up and around soon."

The nine-year-old smiled. "Okay." After Cole finished listening to her lungs, she coughed. "I'm sorry about my dad. Sometimes he can be scary, but he's not. Really."

Sara patted her arm. "I know. He was just worried about you."

"You'll let him keep coming to see us, won't you?"

Sara raised her eyebrow at Cole and immediately saw resignation in his eyes. "As long as he behaves, no one will stop him from visiting," Cole answered, his gaze meeting Sara's.

"Promise?" Mandy asked.

"I promise."

"We're finished, so you can rest," Sara told her. "Meanwhile, we'll send in your parents, okay?"

Mandy nodded as she closed her eyes. "Okay."

Outside the room, Cole stripped off his protective wear. "Hell," he muttered.

"What's wrong?"

"I was looking forward to watching Security escort him from the premises."

Her husband wore a distinctly disgruntled expression, much like a little boy who'd plotted some misdeed only to have his plan thwarted at the last minute. "But now you can't," she reminded him. "If you do, you'll have one upset nine-year-old."

He ran a hand through his hair. "I know. Do you have any idea how worried I was?"

She smiled. "I think so, but I had the situation under control."

He snorted. "Yeah, right. Guys like that usually have trouble with their tempers, which means that I may get to see Security in action after all. His presence in the hospital *is* contingent on good behavior."

"Cut him some slack, Cole. The man's worried about his kids. If you were in his shoes—if Brody were lying in that bed—wouldn't you take on the world for him?"

He frowned. "I guess so. When I saw him threaten you—"

"He didn't hurt me," she assured him.

"Well, I'd feel better if you didn't go into that room alone when he's there."

"Trust me, Cole. He'll be on his best behavior. His wife will see to it. Besides, he loves his kids and if he knows—which he does now—that if he steps out of line, he won't be able to see them, he'll be motivated to stay calm."

"Let's hope so."

She grinned at him. "Now go and be nice to the Bertons while I phone the pharmacy with your new drug orders."

"You don't want to join me to make sure *I* behave?"

"I could, but we want to show Tom that we're attacking Mica's medical condition aggressively. That means the sooner we start the new antibiotic, the better."

"Okay, but just so you know, I plan to stick around this ward as much as I can. To keep an eye on things," he muttered darkly.

She smiled at his protective streak, deciding this wasn't a good time to point out she'd encountered far more antagonistic patients than Tom Berton and had lived to tell the tale. "As much as I appreciate your coming to my rescue…" she rested her hand on his arm and noticed the tension underneath the layers of clothing "…we—I—will be fine, so don't do it on my account," she said.

He met her gaze and spoke in a serious tone. "Of course I'm doing it for you."

"Oh, Cole," she said, surprised by his blatant protective streak, "were you really worried?"

"Why wouldn't I be? A fellow twice the size of my wife was pushing her around. I had no idea what he'd do next. For all I knew, he intended to throw you through the window."

"He wasn't *that* far out of control."

He raised an eyebrow. "Are you sure?"

In spite of wanting to believe that her calm attitude would have activated Tom's common sense, she wasn't sure.

"I'm sticking around as much as possible," he said in no uncertain terms, "and I'm doing it as much for me as I am for you. Now, we'd both better get to work before Tom gets too impatient and comes looking for us."

For the rest of the afternoon, Sara was certain she walked around her ward with a goofy expression of surprise, but it wasn't because Cole was true to his word and had a very visible presence so she'd feel safe. Neither was she surprised by his obvious concern. As he'd pointed out, Tom wasn't a featherweight and an angry male could be a dangerous force to be reckoned with.

No, what had surprised her the most was that he'd *admitted* to being worried. Had this incident happened a few weeks ago, he would have been just as protective, but he'd never have confessed to needing peace of mind for himself.

There was hope for him yet.

CHAPTER EIGHT

IF COLE lived to be a hundred, he'd never forget Sara's expression after he'd announced his reasons for not letting her out of his proverbial sight. If he'd been thinking more clearly at the time, he would have simply called Security and asked them to patrol the ward, but he hadn't.

He also could have hung around under the guise of monitoring the Berton children, but he hadn't done that either. Instead, he'd blurted out what he'd really been feeling.

To his own surprise, the sky hadn't fallen, the earth hadn't trembled, his tongue hadn't snapped off its rollers and Sara hadn't made fun of him. Instead, she had looked as happy as she had on the day he'd finally proposed, and that happiness seemed to carry her for the next week.

Did he really hold that much of himself back, especially from his own wife? If so, he truly needed to make a few personal changes, especially if the rewards would be so great.

However, a few days later, when Sara had tentatively announced her upcoming doctor's appointment, his own response made it obvious that he'd been changing and hadn't realized it…

"I know we'd talked about waiting before we pursued fertility tests," she began, almost apologetically, "but the opportunity presented itself and I just couldn't pass it up. And it isn't like we're going gangbusters on this. It's only a physical, Cole. When life with Brody has settled down and he's adjusted, we'll do something, but until then…please don't be angry—"

Cole interrupted her breathy explanation with a short kiss. While he was a little disappointed that she'd taken this step on her own, he understood about seizing opportunities. And now that Brody had enriched their lives, he discovered he wasn't as reluctant to eventually add to their household as he once had been.

"It's okay," he told her. "You don't have to explain. I'm not angry."

"Truly?" she asked, the worry in her eyes lessening.

"Truly. If a physical will give you peace of mind, then that's what we should do," he said firmly, certain a doctor's report would chase away her doubts and restore some badly needed confidence in this area of her life. Considering everything she'd done for him, this seemed like the least he could do for her.

However, as they sat in Josh Eller's office a few days later, she was anything but peaceful...

"Nervous?" Cole asked as she thumbed through her third magazine in less than five minutes.

She flashed him a half smile. "Silly of me, isn't it?"

"No, but worrying won't change anything."

"I know." Her chuckle was weak. "It's just that I'm torn between hoping he found something abnormal and hoping that he didn't."

"Don't look for trouble," he advised. "Chances are everything is fine and you're worrying for nothing."

"Let's hope so."

"Mrs. Wittman?"

As soon as the nurse called her name, Sara exhaled once, smiled at him tremulously, then rose. "You're coming, aren't you?" she turned back to ask him.

His wife was obviously giving him permission to sit in on her exam, so he jumped to his feet. "Of course."

For the next thirty minutes, he chatted with Josh as the ob-gyn checked Sara from the top of her head to the soles of her feet. As soon as he'd finished, he ushered Cole into his office where they talked of inconsequential things until Sara rejoined them.

"Your physical exam was unremarkable," Eller told them. "I didn't expect it to be otherwise. Your basic lab results were also within the established reference ranges."

"That's good, isn't it?" she asked.

"It is. However…" he shuffled a few papers on his desk "…we also ran a few hormone assays and one result stood out." He placed the page in front of them so they could both review it.

The FSH result was in bold-faced print with an *H* beside it, indicating it was higher than normal.

"As you can see," Eller continued, "the level of FSH, or follicle-stimulating hormone, is elevated."

Sara glanced at Cole and he steeled his face into impassive lines to hide his dismay. "Which means what?" she asked.

"As Cole can tell you, FSH does what its name implies—it stimulates the growth of immature ovarian follicles."

"But that's good, isn't it?"

"If the level is high in the first days of a woman's cycle, yes. But then, as a follicle grows, other hormones kick in to stimulate maturation and then these in turn suppress the FSH. Based on what Sara told me, high levels of FSH at this time in her cycle indicate that this restricting feedback mechanism is either absent or impaired."

"Are you saying that Sara is menopausal?" Cole asked.

Menopausal? Fear struck Sara's heart. That couldn't be. It just couldn't...

"I'm not saying anything," Josh said. "While premature menopause is a possibility, at her age it could also indicate she has poor ovarian reserve, which is a fancy term to describe a woman's chance for conceiving. Because women are born with all the eggs they're going to have, we have to assess if the elevated FSH level is due to a decreased number of eggs or some other hormonal condition that is interfering with the normal feedback mechanism."

"Would IVF be a solution for us?" Cole asked.

"It might be," he admitted, "and it might not. So much depends on properly diagnosing the cause of your infertility. However, the fact that she'd been pregnant before suggests that structurally there isn't a problem. Because the FSH is elevated and is the most obvious issue, we'll focus our attention down that path."

Then she still had hope… "If in vitro fertilization is the answer, then how did I get pregnant the first time?"

Eller smiled. "What can I say? The conditions must have been just right. In any case, IVF would simply increase your chances of achieving pregnancy, but before we rush you to an IVF facility, we'll run a lot more tests, including a sperm count on you, Cole."

"More tests?" Sara asked, trying to remember what she'd learned during her nursing-school days.

"We'll start with the clomiphene citrate challenge test. This procedure will indicate how well you'll respond to induced ovulation and is the best predictor of ovarian reserve that we have at the moment."

"What's involved?" she asked.

"On day two or three of your next menstrual cycle, we'll draw a blood sample for another baseline FSH level and perform a transvaginal ultrasound. On day five, you'll begin taking the clomiphene citrate tablets and continue for five days through day nine. Then on day ten or eleven, we'll draw blood for another FSH level."

Sara glanced at Cole. "Sounds simple enough."

"And this will give us the answers we need," Cole stated, as if asking for confirmation.

"Yes and no. This test is merely a predictor. If the results are abnormal, a very poor chance of pregnancy is predicted. Studies have shown that these women respond poorly to injectable fertility drugs, have fewer eggs retrieved for IVF, lower pregnancy and higher miscarriage rates, and an increased risk for chromosomally abnormal embryos. Which is why many fertility programs use this test to screen prospective IVF patients to eliminate those with odds against their success."

"And if the results are normal?" Sara asked, her tone hopeful.

"Unfortunately, normal FSH levels during this challenge test don't tell us anything. A normal result doesn't *prove* your ovaries are working well and therefore the test won't predict that you *will* get pregnant. This is confusing, I know."

"Then why run the test?"

"Because predicting what *won't* work saves a lot of stress and heartache on everyone, especially the couple, for the reasons I mentioned earlier. And if you can screen out those who don't have good odds, you can save them a huge financial burden as well."

"In other words, an abnormal result identifies patients with poor ovarian reserve," Cole clarified.

"Exactly. Then these couples can pursue other options. But before we debate the predictive value and your candidacy in an IVF program, let's see what the test reveals. No sense in getting ahead of ourselves."

Eller addressed Sara. "You're close to your next period, aren't you?" At her nod, he added, "Then we can either arrange to perform this test at your next cycle, or we can wait until next month, after the holidays are over. Or we can wait to continue until you're both ready to add to your family."

Sara exchanged a glance with Cole, uncertain about what to do next.

"Can we have a few minutes to discuss this?" Cole asked Josh.

"Of course."

As soon as Josh closed the door behind him, Cole faced Sara. "What do you want to do?"

Her smile was weak and she plucked at some

imaginary lint on her pants. "Logically, we should wait. Brody is still adapting and we've just recently ironed out our own differences. Maybe we should just be satisfied with the three of us as a family."

"But you'd still like to know for certain."

She met his gaze. "Yes, I would."

"Then it's settled." As he rose to summon Josh into the room, she stopped him.

"I don't want you to feel pressured."

He bent down and kissed her forehead. "I don't. In fact, the idea of giving Brody a brother or a sister isn't as frightening as it once was, thanks to you."

She searched his face for the truth. "Really?"

He smiled. "Really."

Six months, even six weeks ago, Sara would have taken his words at face value and blithely continued on, believing Cole's reticence was because he was a man of few words.

Then Brody had come along and his presence had forced her see her husband in a new light. While she'd demanded that Cole change and bring more openness and honesty to their relationship—and he was making progress—she had changed, too. She'd become more cognizant of when his mood didn't quite match his remarks, and less inclined to take situations and comments at face value. And right now his smile didn't quite reach his eyes, which suggested he had a few worries.

"But you have reservations," she continued.

He paused, brow furrowed, as if weighing his words. "I suppose I do," he finally admitted. "Not because we don't love each other enough to handle another baby but because couples can get so caught up with trying to get pregnant that it interferes with the rest of their family life."

His concern suddenly seemed so obvious she didn't know why she hadn't seen it before.

"This won't detract from our first Christmas with Brody," she assured him. "He won't miss any of the usual holiday festivities and I won't deprive him of any of our family traditions. We'll do everything we'd normally do at this time of year and more."

She made her promise with sincere determination, but at the same time she hoped and prayed for a breakthrough with the little boy who didn't want her to be his mother.

Although Cole didn't mention it, he was relieved to see that Sara had followed through on her promise to make Brody's first Christmas in their home special. He watched as she decorated the house, baked cookies and made candy. They took him to ride the holiday train at the mall where a pretty young elf snapped his picture as he sat on Santa's lap. When the first snowfall came, as the weatherman had predicted, Sara ushered Brody outside so he could catch snowflakes for the first time.

The little boy's wide eyes clearly showed his wonderment as he took in these new sights and experiences but, in spite of Sara's efforts, he still treated her with wariness.

"I know I should be patient," she revealed during one particularly trying afternoon when Brody refused to let her change his wet diaper. "He tolerates me doing things for him if he and I are alone, but if anyone else is here, especially you, then he won't have anything to do with me."

Cole studied his son, wishing the little boy would give Sara a chance to be the mother she so desperately wanted to be. If only he didn't feel so powerless. "Maybe he's just experiencing the normal terrible twos."

She shook her head. "I don't think so. It's more deep-seated than that. It's like he's focusing his anger at the world on me and I don't know how I can help him channel it in another direction. I think we need professional help."

"Okay," he said slowly, "if that's what you think, we can certainly pursue that idea. And maybe it's a matter of you expecting too much from him too soon."

"He doesn't have a problem with you," she pointed out.

"No, but in his mind I wasn't replacing his mother. You are."

She heaved a great sigh. "I guess. I only want…" Her voice died.

"Want what?" he coaxed.

"I want him to need me," she said simply.

He stared at her, incredulous. "Of course he needs you. He's only two, going on three."

"I'm not talking about caregiving. I'm talking about *emotionally* needing me. When he's upset or tired, he goes off by himself, even though I'm right *here*."

"He will. Give him time." He pulled her against him. "You'll see."

Her smile wobbled. "I suppose. It's just that I feel like I'm failing at the most important job I could ever have—the job that Ruth should have had. And if I can't do my job with Brody, what makes me think I could be a mother to anyone else, even my own baby? Maybe we should just forget the test Josh suggested."

"It's my turn to give the pep talk," he told her kindly. "You aren't failing at anything. This is only a rough patch."

"Yeah, right. A rough patch."

He sensed she didn't believe him. "As for your lab test, you don't want to give up so soon, do you?"

She rubbed the back of her neck. "Not really, no."

"Then just be patient." Then, because she didn't seem to welcome his advice, he asked, "Have you ever read Ruth's letter?"

"No."

"Why not? You might gain an entirely new perspective on what makes Brody tick."

"Maybe," she said, her tone noncommittal.

"Then you'll read it?" he coaxed.

She nodded. "Someday. When I'm ready."

"Don't wait too long," he cautioned. "For all you know, she had a few tips to make his adjustment easier." Then, sensing he wouldn't help his cause by pushing too hard, he traced her mouth with his thumb. "You know what you need at this very moment?"

"A kiss?" she asked hopefully.

He grinned before he planted a long, lingering one on her mouth. "Besides that."

"I can't imagine."

"You," he said as he tugged her to the mud room directly off the kitchen, "need some fresh air."

She laughed, sounding like a schoolgirl. "It's freezing outside."

"It's thirty-one," he said, "which makes it perfect snowman-building weather."

"You've got to be kidding."

"I'm not. You can't build snowmen if it's warm enough for shirtsleeves. There won't be any of the white stuff."

"Yes, but—"

"No arguments. I'll get Brody while you find things to make their faces and accessorize."

"Faces?" she asked. "As in plural? I thought we were only making one snowman."

He shrugged. "One, three, who's counting? We'll see how many we can create before our noses and toes get cold."

"But I have so much to do—" she began.

"It can wait," he informed her. "Making the first Wittman snow family can't."

"Is he asleep already?" Sara asked as Cole dropped onto his easy chair later that evening.

"Oh, yeah. After you finished his story and left the room, I only read as far as the third page of his second book before he closed his eyes. He had a busy day today."

"I'll say," she said. "Building a snow family is hard work." She thought of the trio they'd created. The biggest was Papa Snowman, as Cole had called him, and he sported a disreputable baseball cap on his round head. Mama Snowman was smaller, with a long strip of fabric around her neck to act as a muffler. Baby Snowman was Brody-size and without adornment until Brody had shaken his head and demanded a cap "like Daddy's."

Fortunately, when Cole had named the family—Daddy, Mama and Baby—Brody hadn't objected. He'd posed happily beside *his* snowman for one of the many photos that Sara had taken.

To Sara's further delight, he'd joined her in making snow angels and had even gone so far as to grab her hand and tell her "More" when he wanted her to help him cover the yard with them.

Maybe she *was* making progress…

"Did you get any good pictures?" he asked.

"More than enough," she answered, mentally reviewing the digital images of Brody giggling, his little cheeks rosy from the cold as he played in the snow. His red stocking hat drooped over his eyes and his matching mittens were caked with snow, but his smile stretched from ear to ear and his eyes sparkled with excitement.

And, of course, there was Cole, looking at his son with a benevolent air as he rolled a giant snowball and explained the finer points of his technique to a little boy who was more hindrance than help.

To think that Cole had been afraid he wasn't father material… As far as Sara was concerned, Brody could have none better.

An image of the one very special garment she hadn't ever worn popped into her head. Suddenly feeling rejuvenated, she dropped her magazine on the coffee table and rose.

"I'm going to take a shower," she said, "and go to bed."

Concern crossed his face. "This early?"

She smiled her best come-hither smile. "I didn't say anything about *sleeping,* did I? Unless, of course, you're too tired?" She raised an eyebrow.

His eyes sparkled with enthusiasm. "Me? Tired? Not a chance."

Sara tiptoed down the hall to their bedroom and after digging through a drawer and turning the contents into a jumbled mess she pulled out the teddy in a flurry of silk and lace. Then she hurried into the bathroom with her lingerie and her plans to make this an evening to remember.

When she came out of the bathroom twenty minutes later, Cole was lounging on top of the bed, obviously waiting for her.

A slow, feral grin spread across his face as he rose with the same grace as a jungle cat and approached her. "You look…fantastic."

"Thanks," she answered, pleased by his obvious delight, "but it seems to me you're overdressed."

"Not for long," he answered as he reached for her. "Not for long."

Cole woke up early the next morning blissfully content. As he reached instinctively for Sara, he was surprised to find her missing. Not only that, her side of the bed was cold, as if she'd been gone for hours. After the night of loving they'd had, he couldn't believe she'd left their cozy nest.

He was disappointed, too, because he would have loved to start their morning in a very special way...

Curious, he slipped on his bathrobe and padded out of the room to find her.

The last of his mental cobwebs disappeared as soon as he discovered Brody's empty room.

Thanks to the streetlight's glow streaming through the window, he found Sara on the sofa, spooned protectively around his son.

The sight made him smile.

Sara would wake up stiff and sore from her cramped position, he was certain. He debated the wisdom of carrying Brody to his own bed, but they seemed so comfortable together that he hated to disturb either of them. If he'd needed proof that Brody was on the verge of accepting Sara, this was it.

Seeing one of her feet had escaped the comforter, he tucked it around her toes and covered them with an extra afghan for good measure.

She stirred. "What time is it?" she whispered.

"Four-thirty," he told her. "Do you want me to put him in his own bed?"

"No," she murmured. "We'll end up back here anyway. He'll wake soon enough."

She talked as if this had happened often enough to establish a pattern. He was surprised he hadn't realized what had been happening under his own nose, but now that he did, he intended to grill her for details. At a decent hour, of course.

"Good night," she added sleepily.

Feeling oddly left out, he returned to his own cold bed. Although the sensation of being on the outside looking in wasn't new to him—his childhood had been full of those moments—this was the first time he'd experienced it with Brody.

As he lay there, he thought about the woman who'd wanted to be needed since she was a little girl. No wonder Sara struggled with the little boy's rejection, and no wonder she savored these nighttime moments when Brody's subconscious allowed him to accept her mothering. While he was glad their relationship was improving, even if only on such an elemental level, at this moment only one thought bounced around his head.

He was jealous of his own son.

* * *

"How long have you two been sleeping on the sofa?" Cole asked Sara the next morning over coffee.

Sara smiled as she liberally poured in sweetener and creamer. She'd anticipated this conversation from the moment she'd woken up and put Brody back in his own bed.

"I'm not sure. A week. Ten days, maybe," she answered. "It began one night when I heard him crying and found him in the living room. Every time I put him back in his bed, he'd eventually gravitate back to the sofa. I could have left him alone out there, but it didn't seem right." She sipped her coffee, hoping the warm drink would ease the familiar achy feeling in her abdomen.

"So you stayed with him."

"It seemed the only way either of us would get any sleep," she said simply.

"You could have brought him to bed with us."

"I could have," she admitted, "but he always gravitates to the sofa, so I thought it best to share it with him."

"We need to think of a different solution," he said. "Neither of you are getting a good night's sleep."

She flexed her arms and moved her head to

ease the kinks in her neck. "Tell me about it," she said dryly. "But what choice do we have?"

"We should have retired his toddler bed and gotten a regular bed when he moved in," he said.

"If you recall, we wanted to surround him with as many familiar things as possible," she reminded him. "New furniture could wait, you said."

"That was before we had this problem. Now we're going to sell him on the idea of having a big-boy bed, like his mommy and daddy have."

"I'm not sure he's ready for that sort of change," she began slowly.

"We have to do something," he pointed out. "Continuing like this isn't an option."

He sounded so forceful that Sara smiled. "What happened? Did you miss me?"

"Always," he growled as he hugged her. "Then it's settled. We'll shop for a new bed and if he needs company because he's afraid or had a nightmare, we can join him there instead of on the sofa."

"A little behavior modification."

"Precisely." He smiled. "It's what you're already practicing on him so it should be easy to take matters a step further."

She stifled a yawn. "It's worth a try.

As it turned out, Brody began to wander into their room during his sleepwalking episodes. They took turns carrying him back to his room where they spent what remained of the night in his bed. Sometimes they simply allowed him to climb between them.

However, no matter what they did, he'd heave a sigh—of relief, perhaps, or maybe it was contentment—as she cuddled him close. Idly, she wondered if he'd ever climbed into bed with his mother, but that was something else she'd never know.

Immediately the letter Ruth had written came to mind, but she couldn't bring herself to read it. Not because she didn't want to potentially gain insights into Brody's first two years of life, but because she didn't want to risk reading that Ruth had been in love with her husband all this time or that his version of events wasn't quite as he'd explained. She was certain they had been—at least from Cole's point of view—but why dwell on the past and introduce unnecessary doubts?

So Sara continued to do what she always did and left the letter on top of their dresser, unopened.

A few days later, Sara began her clomiphene citrate challenge test with a combination of disappointment and relief—disappointment that she hadn't gotten pregnant on her own and relief that they were taking matters into their own hands. However, by the time the ten-day protocol ended, cautious optimism had taken hold. She also suffered from moments of dread, but she swiftly pushed those out of her head. Not knowing the truth was worse than knowing, she'd decided, and she was eager for answers.

"Are you ready for Christmas?" Eller's nurse asked her as she drew Sara's final blood sample during Sara's lunch hour.

"I think so," Sara answered. "Goodies are made, presents are under the tree and the house is ready for guests. The only problem I have now is keeping everyone healthy. Our son—" she still found it difficult to refer to Brody as such "—developed the sniffles and I'm hoping he'll fight off his cold before the holidays are upon us."

"At this time of year, it's tough," the nurse commiserated. "Unfortunately, we seem to be passing our germs back and forth at my house and winter has only begun. Spring can't come soon enough for me." She taped a cotton ball over the puncture site on Sara's arm. "That's it for now. We'll see you in five days for your follow-up appointment."

Offering her thanks, Sara left, taking a detour to the hospital cafeteria for a carton of yogurt before returning to her ward.

Georgia, the ward clerk, immediately stopped her. "Your husband signed out the Berton kids while you were gone."

"He did? That's great." The two children had made remarkable progress over the past few days. The change she'd seen from the last shift she'd worked until today had been phenomenal, thanks to the miracle of antibiotics. "Did he say anything about Mrs. VanMeter?"

Dorothy had been off-color that morning, although Sara couldn't point to anything concrete that would account for it. Her vital signs were good, she wasn't having trouble breathing or had any unusual pain, but something wasn't quite right. She'd hoped Cole would see what she was missing.

Georgia shook her head. "Not to me. You might ask one of the other nurses, though."

"I will. First, though, I'll see about sending the Bertons home. As busy as this place is, it won't take long to fill an empty bed."

As expected, Mica and Mandy were delighted to be leaving the hospital. Although they weren't completely recovered, they were definitely on the road to recovery.

As soon as she took care of all the paperwork and discussed the list of dos and don'ts, she accompanied them to their car and waved goodbye. Afterward, she went directly to Dorothy's room.

"How are you feeling?" Noting that her patient's coloring was still off, she automatically took her pulse.

"Oddly enough, not good," Dorothy admitted. "My chest and my back feel strange."

This was the first time the woman had mentioned a specific symptom. "Did you tell Dr. Wittman about this?"

"No, because I just started feeling like this a few minutes ago."

Sara immediately dug her phone out of her pocket and texted Cole, smiling all the while so as not to let Dorothy see her concern. "I'm sure it's nothing, but let's get the doctor back in here, shall we?"

Dorothy nodded. "Okay. By the way, I've been thinking. Would you mind calling my kids for me?"

Remembering how Dorothy had mentioned

her kids were actually her stepchildren and her contact with them was minimal, Sara was half-surprised by the request. "I'd be happy to," she said. "Do we have their phone numbers?"

"I gave them to the lady when I checked in at the front desk."

"Then they're probably in your computer records. I'll look and if the numbers aren't there, I'll come back."

"Okay," Dorothy said. "My address book is in my handbag if you need it."

"Is there anything specific you'd like me to tell them?" Sara asked kindly.

"No, just that I'm still in the hospital. And that I'm sorry—" Suddenly, Dorothy clutched her chest and her head rolled limply to one side.

Sara immediately ran around the bed to grab the phone and punch 0 for the operator. After a terse and well-rehearsed message, she hung up. Without hesitation and only a few seconds later, she lowered the head of the bed and began cardiac compressions just as the disembodied voice came over the hospital loudspeaker.

"Code blue, room 412."

CHAPTER NINE

AFTER receiving his text summons to room 412, Cole was on his way when the announcement blared out of the speakers. Muttering a curse, he raced down the hall, up the stairs and burst into the room, not surprised that Sara and two other nurses were already at work.

"Status?" he barked.

Someone called out the most recent blood-pressure reading while another nurse was forcing air into Dorothy's lungs via an Ambu bag. Sara, meanwhile, was performing chest compressions with enough vigor to produce a sheen on her forehead.

"Still no pulse," a voice supplied.

"Okay, Sara," he said, "step aside. We'll defibrillate."

Another pair of hands slapped the paddles into his and as soon as he yelled "Clear," a jolt of electricity surged into Dorothy's body. The heart monitor, which had previously shown a flat line, now showed the characteristic blip they'd wanted to achieve.

"BP is one-ten over seventy and rising."

"Let's get labs and move her into CCU," he added. "Good job, everyone."

As soon as Dorothy was wheeled away, with an oxygen mask covering her face, Cole stopped Sara. "I presume you were here at the time of her MI?"

She nodded. "I'd come in to check on her because I didn't like the way she looked, which was why I'd texted you."

"I was on my way when the code blue was announced."

"Anyway, we were talking and she asked me to contact her kids. She's never asked me to do that before and as far as I know, none of them have ever come to see her. Regardless, she'd asked me to give them a message and then she collapsed. I immediately called the code and began chest compressions."

"You probably saved her life," he said. "If she was going to have a coronary, she had excellent timing to have one while you were in the room."

She smiled, clearly pleased by his praise. "Well, thanks. Let's hope her family feels the same way."

"Do you want me to call them?"

She thought a moment. "As tempting as it is, I'll do it. If they want more information, then you can call them later, after you see her settled in CCU."

"Okay." He hesitated. "How did the blood test go this morning?"

She rubbed the bend of her elbow and felt the wad of cotton underneath her long-sleeved shirt. "Like any blood test," she said. "One prick and it was over. All that's left now is the waiting."

He grinned. "Then that's what we'll do." Although he'd made light of it, he also knew that waiting was often the most difficult part.

Sara entered the house after work, exhausted from the day's hectic pace. She was pleased, however, to find Cole feeding Brody, although she wasn't happy with his choice.

"Fast food?" She raised an eyebrow. "I had our dinner in the refrigerator. All you had to do was heat it."

He chucked Brody under his chin as the little boy shoved four French fries into his mouth at once and grinned. "Ah, but this sounded so much better to our tummies, didn't it, my man?"

Brody wrinkled his nose and tried to shove another fry into his still-full mouth. His little cheeks resembled a chipmunk's from all the food he was trying to chew.

"Cole," she scolded. "He's going to choke. Brody, spit it out."

The little boy shook his head. "Umph."

"Spit it out," she said firmly.

Once again, he shook his head and tried to swallow. "No."

She heaved a deep sigh, but before she could say a word, Cole broke in, his voice stern. "You heard your mother. Empty your mouth before you eat any more."

Brody complied by spitting most of his food onto the floor.

It was a blatant act of defiance and Sara clenched her hands in her pockets, determined not to lose this battle of wills. "Brody," she said calmly, "you will not spit on the floor again or you will not get ice cream for dessert."

As it was his favorite, she expected him to comply. However, he pursed his lips as if he intended to spew more onto the floor, but before he could, Cole put a finger to Brody's mouth.

"No," he said firmly in a tone that meant business. "No spitting. Do you understand?"

Brody answered with a grin. "Okay," he said with good humor.

"Are you finished eating?" At the little boy's nod, Cole wiped his mouth and freed him from his booster seat.

"Play?" Brody asked.

"Yes, you can play," he answered.

As Brody ran off to do just that, suppressed fury made Sara's voice shake. "Did you see that?"

"Yeah. He definitely has an ornery streak."

"Yes, and you just rewarded him for it by letting him play."

He raised an eyebrow. "What would you have him do? Sit in the corner for an hour? Write 'I shall not spit' a hundred times?"

"Of course not," she snapped.

"This isn't like you to get upset over something this minor," he said evenly. "Have a seat and tell me what's *really* bothering you."

"That," she said, pointing to the booster seat, "is what is bothering me. Didn't you see what he did, *after* I told him not to?"

"He's testing you, that's all."

"That's all? That's *all?*" She raised her voice,

irritated that Cole dismissed her concerns so easily.

"I've been doing some thinking about the situation and I came up with an idea that seems to fit. In his eyes, his mother left and never returned and now there's a new person in his life who's supposed to take her place. He's pushing you to see if you'll disappear, too."

"And why doesn't he treat you with the same mistrust?"

"Because he never had a dad before. I'm an extra, not a replacement."

"That's rather high-level thinking for a child his age, isn't it?"

He shrugged. "He may not consciously have plotted his actions, but kids sense more things than we might think. Two-year-olds normally begin testing the limits at their age, so why can't we assume he's expanded those limits to include you?"

Whether Cole was right or not, his theory sounded plausible. Could it be as simple as Cole described?

"Brody's actions aren't the real problem, are they?" he asked. "You normally don't freak out because we stopped at a burger place on our way home. What gives?"

Sara sat, chagrined that she'd overreacted. "I'm in a bad mood, I guess."

"Over what?"

"A lot of things." She paused. "No, mainly one. I phoned Dorothy's children. Stepchildren," she corrected.

"Your call didn't go well, I presume."

Sara shook her head. "One never answered the phone. The son was rude and told me not to bother him again. The third, a daughter, was more polite, but she basically told me that Dorothy wasn't a part of her family. Even when I shared…" Her voice cracked and she cleared her throat. "Dorothy asked me to tell them that she was sorry, but neither of the two I spoke to responded positively. The son laughed and suggested that she was only trying to appease her conscience before she went to meet her Maker."

"Any idea on what she was sorry for?"

She shook her head. "None. Oh, Cole. I feel so badly for that woman. To be her age, sick and nearly dying, and know that you're alone has to be depressing."

"You don't know the circumstances," he pointed

out. "Blended families are hard to create. For all you know, she might have been the worst step-mother in the world."

"She might also have tried her best."

"That's true, but the point is you can't measure their experience against your frame of reference. Families like yours are more rare than you can imagine."

"I know. I keep telling myself that."

"As sweet as Dorothy seems now, she may have been a real shrew and those kids couldn't wait to leave. Abuse comes in many forms," he added soberly. "So don't judge them too harshly until you hear their side of the story."

"I've been telling myself that all afternoon, but you aren't going to be the one who tells Dorothy that her family doesn't care if she lives or dies."

"Don't take it personally," he told her. "You did what your patient asked and if her family doesn't respond, it isn't your fault. Your responsibility ended when you made contact. As they say, the ball is in their court."

"I know." She sighed as she met Cole's gaze. "It's just so *hard* not to try and fix what's broken."

"Yeah, but the trick is knowing what can be repaired and what can't."

She thought of his own family relationships. "What would you do if you got a call about your aunt? That she was sick and or dying and wanted to see you?"

"I'd like to think I'd be a bigger man and would meet her one last time," he mused, "but, honestly, I don't know what I'd do until I was faced with that situation. With all the bad feelings between us, I'd probably be just as disinterested as Dorothy's stepchildren are."

She'd suspected as much. Given the few stories he'd shared with her, she couldn't fault him for that decision. "I have to admit, the whole stepmother-stepchildren relationship is frightening."

"How so?"

"Of the three families I know with that sort of family dynamics—yours, Dorothy's and now ours with Brody—do you realize two of those situations turned out badly? Given those odds, what sort of chance do we have for success? Brody already thinks of me as the enemy. Will he eventually hate me, too? I don't want him to grow up so scarred that his future relationships suffer because of it."

There, she'd said it. She'd finally voiced the worry that had plagued her all afternoon. The idea of someday being alone to face a serious illness without family support sent a cold shudder down her spine.

"Sara," he chided gently, "you have nothing to fear. I can't speak for Dorothy, but you are not like my aunt by any stretch of the imagination."

"Yes, but maybe she'd tried to reach out to you, too, and you didn't realize—"

"I was old enough to see what my aunt was doing and I was also old enough to understand the vitriol she spewed at me for years as well as on the day I left. You, on the other hand, are as loving as any mother could possibly be."

"Brody might not agree with you," she said darkly.

"Of course he does. If he truly was afraid of you and hated you, he wouldn't try to push your buttons. He certainly wouldn't be happy sleeping beside you at night, but he is, so don't be so hard on yourself."

"It's hard not to," she admitted.

"Try," he ordered kindly. "My psychiatry skills are a little weak, but in my opinion he's only trying to decide if he can trust you to stick around. When he decides that you will, when he realizes that he can't push you away, he won't ever question your role in his life."

She wanted to believe him.

Cole threaded his arm around her waist. "You'll see I'm right. Just be patient."

Patience seemed to be the answer for everything. It was a word she was beginning to hate.

Two days later, Sara stopped by CCU during her lunch break to check on Dorothy. "Has any of her family come by or phoned to check on her?" she asked one of the nurses.

The other woman shook her head. "Not that I'm aware."

"Okay, thanks. How's she doing?"

"So-so. She's somewhat depressed, which isn't unusual in heart patients. The good news is that her tests don't show any residual damage. You may have her back on your floor in a day or two."

Pleased that Dorothy was doing well, physically at least, Sara wondered if her depression was partly due to her family's lack of interest. As Sara couldn't drag Dorothy's stepchildren to visit and she was certainly a poor substitute, she could at least pop in and let her know that someone cared.

"Thanks for stopping by, dearie," Dorothy said,

looking far more frail than she had two days earlier. "I appreciate your concern."

"It's my pleasure," she said cheerfully. "I hear you're doing so well you might be back on our unit before long."

"So I hear," Dorothy said.

Sara talked of non-consequential things for a few more minutes, then, conscious of Dorothy's flagging energy, she left.

Back on her ward, she ran into Cole. "Where've you been?" he asked, sounding curious.

"I went to see Dorothy. Oh, Cole, it's so sad. I know she'd feel better if her children came to visit."

"You don't know that for certain," he countered.

"No, but it couldn't hurt," she insisted. "I wish there was something I could do…"

"Don't meddle in affairs you don't know anything about," he advised. "What if they came and were hateful toward her? Do you really think she needs that right now? Can you risk it?"

She hadn't considered they might be more of a hindrance than a help but, given their attitudes on the phone, it was entirely possible. As Cole had suggested, she couldn't risk upsetting Dorothy. "No, I can't."

Even so, there had to be something she could do…

The next afternoon, Sara was at home with a fussy Brody, trying to find ways to amuse him, when the phone rang.

"We had a cancellation for a three o'clock appointment," Eller's nurse told her. "Would you be interested in taking that spot instead of coming in on Friday?"

"You have the lab results already?" Sara asked, thrilled by the news.

"Yes, and Doctor would like to discuss them with you today, if you're free."

"We'll be there," she promised. Then, after disconnecting the call, she swung Brody around in her delight. "Did you hear that, buddy? They have my results. Oh, dear. We have to find a sitter, don't we? And I have to call your dad."

She dialed Cole's number, but he didn't answer, so she left a message. Then, knowing Millie was off duty today, she phoned her, and thankfully her friend agreed to watch Brody. With child care organized, she tried Cole's phone again. When he didn't answer this time, she called Georgia because he spent quite a bit of his time on her floor.

"He's really swamped today," the ward clerk told her, "but the next time I see him, I'll tell him you called."

Sara hated to go to her appointment without Cole, but what choice did she have? Waiting for an extra two days seemed like unnecessary punishment. Today patience wasn't a part of her vocabulary.

Cole read the text message on his phone and his heart sank. If only he'd read it earlier, but he'd been so busy that he hadn't heard the distinctive ring tone telling him he had a text.

Cancellation at Eller's office. Meet me there at three if you can.

It was four o'clock now, which meant that he'd missed the appointment. He hated knowing that Sara had gone without him because, whether she heard good news or bad, she'd have to deal with it alone when that was news best handled together.

He half expected her to come by the hospital, but she didn't.

When he tried to phone her, his call went straight to her voice mail.

He tried not to jump to conclusions, aware that not being able to reach her could mean anything, but he was quick to leave when his shift ended.

As he pulled into the driveway, the lights in the house were on and the Christmas lights hanging from the guttering twinkled as usual. He walked in, and found her sitting at the kitchen table, watching Brody chase his sliced hot dogs and macaroni across his plate.

"Sara," he said, "I'm so sorry I didn't get your message until it was too late. How did your appointment go?"

The minute she raised her head, he saw the red-rimmed eyes and he knew… "Tell me," he said.

"The test was abnormal," she said dully. "Not just a little abnormal, but a lot. My FSH was high."

"How high?"

"High enough that I won't ever have children of my own." She swiped at a single tear trailing down her cheek. "Gosh, I hate this. I've cried buckets all afternoon. You'd think I was cried out by now." She blew her nose for emphasis.

"Is he certain? Absolutely certain?"

"There isn't any doubt. I won't get pregnant on my own and I'm not even a candidate for IVF. According to Eller, my results are such that an IVF facility won't even consider me for the procedure. And if one would, chances are I'd have a low pregnancy success rate—about five percent. He also said that my poor egg quality may have been a factor in my miscarriage."

"Oh, Sara." He scooted a chair close enough so he could hug her. "I'm sorry. I know how much having a baby meant to you, but surely Josh suggested other options."

He had, but she'd been too numb to listen carefully. "He mentioned something about IVF with a donor egg."

"That's good news, isn't it?"

She stared at her husband. "But the baby wouldn't be *mine*."

"Then you won't consider the possibility? Is knowing Brody is my biological son and not yours that big a problem to you?"

"It's not a problem as such," she countered. "I wanted to give you something that no one else could, something that would be yours *and* mine. I wanted our kids to be *ours*."

"Then what are you saying?" he demanded. "If you can't have your own baby, you don't want to be *anyone's* mother?"

Was that what she wanted? "No," she said slowly. "It's just that I pinned my hopes on giving you a *part* of me, but I can't. Knowing that makes me feel so..." she searched for the right words "...inadequate. A failure."

"You are not inadequate *or* a failure." He spoke vehemently. "Absolutely do not say you are."

She met his gaze, her eyes wounded. "What would *you* call not being able to give you a son or a daughter? How would *you* describe it when I can't convince Brody to accept me as his mother? I couldn't even talk an old woman's stepchildren into visiting her after she suffered a heart attack. If those aren't failures, then I don't know what is.

"And to add insult to injury," she added, without giving him an opportunity to interrupt, "of all the health problems I could have had, mine is so elemental that it's part of being a female. And if I'm flawed in that area, then—"

"You are not flawed," he said fiercely. "So your body has a few issues. So Brody is slow at coming around and you couldn't break through three people's stubbornness. You're still a kind, thoughtful woman who has a heart bigger than she is.

"As for giving me something that no one else could, you already have," he said simply. "You've given me your love, your forgiveness and your understanding. Everything else is window dressing."

Touched by his comment, moisture trickled down her cheeks. "Thanks, but—"

"There's no buts about it," he said, moving in close to rest her forehead against his chin. "Those things mean more to me than you'll ever know or understand."

Cole sensed that he hadn't convinced her, probably because she was too mired in her own misery. She was grieving for her lost dreams and wouldn't hear what he had to say until she'd worked through the worst of her sorrow.

No matter. He'd repeat himself until she finally accepted his comments as truth.

The whole problem was that Sara needed to be needed. Even as a child, that had been evident, and recent events had raised those old doubts about her role in her family. It was up to him to convince her that the instances she'd named were simply rocky spots and not utter failures.

"Now," he said with mock consternation, "I want you to focus on all the things I told you—the positives and not the negatives—but the main thing I want you to dwell on is that I need you, Sara. You bring out the best in me. No one else can fill my empty places like you can."

"But, Brody—"

He cut her off. "A strand of thread is just that, a strand, and it's easily broken. However, two strands woven together make a cord that is stronger and more able to handle pressure. Together, we make that cord, Sara, the cord that's held together by mutual love and respect. Together, we'll be the best parents we can be to Brody, which means he needs *us*. Not us as individuals, but us as a team."

"You make it sound so simple."

"It is," he said. "Burdens shared are burdens halved."

For the next few hours, Sara moped. She tried to count her blessings, to look at her situation through rose-colored glasses, but it was a constant battle.

As Brody became more recalcitrant and fussy, she wondered if she was only deluding herself that she had any mothering genes in her at all. However, slowly, but surely, Cole's comments popped into her head periodically.

You are not inadequate or a failure.

You've already given me something that no one else has. You've given me your love, your forgiveness and your understanding. Everything else is window dressing.

I need you, Sara... Together, we're whole.

Slowly, but surely, she accepted what she couldn't change. What she had to do was focus on what she *did* have, and right now she had a very crabby little boy on her hands.

By the next morning, Brody's cold hadn't improved. He'd been running a mild fever and his nose was perpetually congested in spite of her best efforts throughout the night to give him relief. His dry cough had worsened, too, and the combination had made him out of sorts, when he normally woke up bright-eyed and ready to greet the world. To make matters worse, he refused to eat or drink.

The thought of whooping cough occurred to her, but she didn't want to be one of those overreactive mothers who thought her child had caught every disease making the rounds at the time. After all, his records indicated that he only lacked the final booster which was given around age four, so the odds of that particular scenario were slim. Even so, she watched him carefully throughout the morning, monitoring each symptom and weighing it against the previous one.

Unfortunately, by midafternoon she still hadn't been able to coax him to drink his favorite grape juice and he'd grown more listless than she'd ever seen him. After she checked his diaper and found it dry when it normally would have been soaked, she phoned his pediatrician.

"Bring him in," she was told. "We won't know if it's whooping cough without swabbing his nose and throat for culture."

So, with growing concern because he didn't fight the coat and hat routine as he normally did, Sara drove him to the doctor's office.

An hour later, after blood tests that revealed an elevated white blood count as well as dehydration, and an X-ray that—thank goodness—didn't show fluid in his lungs, she was on her way to the hospital, experiencing the inpatient process from the side of the consumer rather than the caregiver.

With a heavy heart, filled with remorse and self-recriminations, she carried Brody to the pediatric wing, accompanied by Amy, a forty-year-old pediatric nurse.

"Room 440 will be yours," Amy mentioned as she led her to the room in question. "There's a sofa that opens into a bed, as well as a rather comfortable recliner for you to use. If you'll have a seat, I'll get my supplies and we'll get the two of you organized."

As she left, Cole strode in, his face lined with worry. "I got your message. What's wrong?"

Relieved to see her husband, she sank onto the recliner with Brody in her arms. "Dr. Keller suspects whooping cough."

Cole stared at her. "You're kidding."

Sara shook her head. "I wish I was. She won't know for certain until the culture report comes back, but she's going to treat him as if that's the problem. The good news is that he doesn't have pneumonia. She would have sent us home with an antibiotic, but he's severely dehydrated and she wants him on IV fluids. Oh, Cole…" Her eyes watered. "This is all my fault."

"How so?"

"I've been so focused on me and my disap-pointments that I didn't notice how sick Brody had gotten. I should have—"

"Stop berating yourself," he told her. "I saw him last night, too. If you're looking to blame someone, blame me. I'm the physician in the house and I dismissed his symptoms, too."

Cole obviously considered himself as much at fault as she did. "Maybe we're both being too hard on ourselves," she admitted. "I really didn't notice a change until this morning and then he seemed to go downhill as the day progressed."

"Thank goodness you were alert," he said fer-vently. "If he does have whooping cough, he'll get antibiotics before he has a chance to develop a secondary infection."

Brody opened his eyes at the sound of Cole's voice, but didn't raise his head off Sara's shoul-der. Cole stroked his son's baby-fine hair with a shaky hand. "Hey, big fella," he crooned. "Aren't you feeling good today?"

Brody's smile was halfhearted and he closed his eyes as if too exhausted to pay attention.

Cole's phone beeped. With movements sug-gesting frustration, he checked the message and mumbled a curse. "I can't stay," he said flatly. "There's a patient—"

Although she wanted Cole with her, his other obligations came first. She offered a tremulous smile. "It's okay. There's no point in both of us watching Brody sleep."

He frowned, then nodded, his expression resigned. "I'll come back when I can."

"We'll be here."

"Call if anything changes," he ordered.

"I will." With Cole gone, Sara felt the need to do *something,* so she helped Amy, the peds nurse, settle Brody into bed. As he was already wearing his footed pajamas, they only had to remove his coat. The worst part came when it was time to start his IV.

"Some of the medical staff want to do the honors themselves when it comes to their own children, but I wouldn't recommend it," Amy said somewhat apologetically. "Right now, he needs to associate you with comfort, not pain."

Sara hadn't considered taking on that task at all and if she had, she would have dismissed the idea immediately. "That's okay. My hands aren't steady enough right now to hit anything smaller than the Alaskan pipeline."

It was a testament to both the nurse's skill and the severity of Brody's illness that he merely flinched when Amy inserted the needle. Afterward, he refused to lie in the strange crib with the tent over it.

"I'll hold him for a while," Sara offered.

"That might be best. Meanwhile, I'll start the vaporizer, which should help soothe his lungs and loosen the respiratory secretions. Although he's getting plenty of fluids now, try to convince him to drink on his own."

"I will."

For the rest of the afternoon Sara held Brody in her lap, mentally willing his health to improve. As she stroked the hair off his hot forehead and heard a couple of carolers in the background, she wondered when Brody had wiggled his way into her heart. As much as she'd resented his origins, now they no longer mattered. He was theirs to nurture and protect, much like another baby had needed nurturing and protecting some two thousand years ago—the same baby who'd eventually become responsible for the Christmas season.

She dozed herself, not realizing the late hour until Cole strode in after his shift had ended, minus his lab coat and tie.

"I'll take him," he said, reaching for Brody. "You need a break."

Although she knew he was right, she handed over the little boy reluctantly. She helped herself to the Popsicles in the ward's kitchenette and watched as Cole painstakingly urged him to eat. After Brody had nibbled away half of it, he closed his eyes and fell asleep again.

"Why don't you go home and rest?" Cole suggested. "I'll stay with him."

She started to protest, realizing she sounded like Mrs. Berton and so many other mothers whose children were in the hospital.

No, that wasn't right. She didn't just *sound* like a mother. She *felt* like one. And if she felt like one, she needed to *act* like one. Mothers did not leave their children.

"Just for a while," Cole coaxed, as if he understood the reason for her hesitation. "An hour or two is all."

An hour. She could do that, even though she really didn't want to go. "Okay."

"Good. Oh, and when you come back, bring something I can lounge in, will you?"

"You're staying, too?"

He nodded. "What would I do in an empty house by myself?"

What indeed? "Do you want dress clothes for tomorrow?" she asked.

He nodded. "I can shower and change in the doctors' lounge before I go on duty."

"I'll be back soon," she promised.

At home, she showered, changed clothes and threw Cole's things into a duffel bag. As she headed out of their bedroom, Ruth's letter caught her eye.

I'm sorry Brody got so ill, she silently murmured. *I should have been paying closer attention.*

But if you had, a little voice asked, *what would you have done?*

The question brought her up short. As a medical professional, she knew doctors didn't intervene just because a child developed a cough or a cold. Even if she'd taken Brody to the doctor yesterday, chances were they would have been sent home to try the home remedies she'd done on her own. Instead of blaming herself, she should do as Cole had suggested. She should be grateful she'd noticed a change when she had.

She would, she vowed. Then, as she took another step forward, her little voice spoke again.

Read the letter.

This isn't the right time, she told herself. She was on her way back to the hospital. Besides, with the disappointments and trials of the past few days, not to mention her struggle with feelings of inadequacy, did she really want to read a message from a dead woman now?

And yet would there *ever* be a good time to hear Ruth's last words?

CHAPTER TEN

UNDECIDED about the wisdom of her actions or her timing, Sara hefted the envelope in her hand. But as she debated, she realized she was tired of having the letter's contents hanging over her head like an ax about to fall. It was now or never.

She dropped the duffel bag onto the floor, sat on the edge of the bed and after a deep breath carefully slid one finger under the sealed flap.

Dear Sara,

If you're reading this, it means that I'm asking a favor of you that I never wanted or planned to ask. I know you must be devastated at the news that Cole is my son's father, but forgive me when I say our choices that night eventually led to the best thing that ever happened to me. I have nothing but the utmost respect for your husband and the few pleasant memories I have of my youth always included Cole.

For what it's worth, Cole could only talk about you during the time we were together. It won't be easy for you to forgive him or me, but for Cole's sake and the sake of his son, I hope you will. You see, the people we really needed weren't there that weekend and consequently we turned to each other, not realizing we would hurt the very ones we loved.

If you're reading this letter, it means I'm not a part of my son's life, which saddens me a great deal. However, I won't regret that Cole could be Brody's father, should you allow him to fill that role. There are many people who would gladly take on this responsibility, but you and Cole are the only ones I'd choose. Cole is a special man—I knew he would be even when we were teenagers—and if he chose you to be his wife, then I know you are just as special. Because of that, and because I believe Brody will need both of you to help him become the kind, caring man I want him to be, I'm asking you to open your heart and let him inside. As wonderful and as strong as your husband is, he can't accomplish this job alone. You, Sara, are the one who has softened Cole's rough edges during the time you've been together and I trust you'll produce the same results with his son. From what Cole has said, I have utmost faith in you.

Time is so short and our lives so fleeting that I hope you'll not only tell Brody every day that I loved him, but that he'll experience a mother's love from you on my behalf. He's the best of both Cole and me, but he's more than that. He's a clean slate, waiting for <u>you</u>—Sara noted the word was underlined—*to write beautiful things on it.*

Someday, perhaps before too much time has passed, you'll have forgiven both of us for the pain we've caused and you'll think on me with fondness.

Sincerely,
Ruth

Sara brushed away the tears on her cheeks. At this moment, she certainly didn't feel like the right woman for the job Ruth had given her, but for all of her faults, flaws and failures, she was the one who was available.

Lost in her thoughts, she returned to the hospital, where she found Brody nestled against Cole as the two men in her life dozed. As she gazed at father and son, love welled up inside her until she thought she might burst. Brody might not share her genetic makeup, but love and acceptance had made him her son, too. Although she'd never implied otherwise, it was an earth-shattering revelation to her and she couldn't wait to share with her husband.

Cole didn't know what startled him awake, but he opened his eyes and saw Sara sitting on the sofa, paging through a magazine. Who would have thought that holding Brody would have made him stiff and sore?

"Have I been sleeping long?" he asked.

She chuckled. "Define long. I've been here for the past hour."

"That's long. What have you been doing?"

"Reading. Making phone calls."

"Phone calls? To your parents?" he guessed.

"And to Dorothy's stepchildren. This time I didn't hold back."

"Oh, my. They won't issue a complaint against you, will they?"

"No, because I didn't call as Dorothy's nurse. I called as her friend. I told them that this was

Christmas and surely they could give Dorothy a chance to make amends."

"Will they?"

She shrugged. "Who knows? If my stirring speech doesn't soften their hearts, then she's better off without them."

"My wife, the crusader." He stirred, shifting Brody in his lap. "He's really a bag of bones, isn't he?"

"Want me to take him?" She dropped her magazine on the seat cushion and rose.

"Let's see how he does in his bed."

Carefully, they maneuvered him into the toddler-size crib. When he didn't stir, merely let out a sigh, they breathed their own sighs of relief.

"Have you had dinner?"

"No." She shook her head. "I brought you a sandwich, though. Ham on rye with extra mustard, just the way you like it."

"Thanks."

As he dug into his food, he watched Sara gaze at Brody. He couldn't define it, but something about her had changed. She seemed more at peace than ever before.

"I am," she admitted when he remarked on it. "Sitting with Brody here in the hospital, worrying about him, made me feel like his mother for the first time."

He grinned. "It took you long enough to figure it out."

"Afraid so. Anyway, I finally realized the biology doesn't matter. Anyone can become a parent, but it's the *parenting* that's most important."

"Wasn't that what I said all along?"

"Yeah, well, I had to figure that out for myself. Afterward, I read Ruth's letter."

"And?"

"She must have been a remarkable woman," she said simply. "I want to help him become the son she'd be proud of."

For all of Sara's efforts, he'd sensed she'd been holding back a part of herself, but now it was as if she'd finally made a firm commitment to the task of raising Brody. He wanted to shout his happiness, but the noise would create a furor on the ward and bring down everyone from code-blue teams to security personnel.

Instead, he abandoned his food and rose to take her into his arms. "You are, without a doubt, the most fantastic woman in the world. I love you."

She grinned. "You are the most fantastic man. And I love you, too, Cole Wittman."

As if on cue, Brody began to fuss. Cole went to the crib and while Sara unlatched and lowered the rail, he reached in to pick him up. To his surprise, Brody shook his head. He said one word as he held out his arms toward Sara.

"Mama."

His wife's eyes immediately filled with tears as she took their son into her embrace. He couldn't imagine a better gift he could have given her on this Christmas Eve.

Christmas Eve, four years later

"MAMA," Brody bellowed at the top of his lungs as he entered the kitchen, where tins of Christmas cookies covered the counter and the air smelled of apples, cranberries and cinnamon. "We're home."

Sara smiled as she greeted him with a smile and a hug that wasn't easy with her growing belly in the way. "I see that," she said softly. "But can you please use your inside voice? Alison is sleeping."

Alison was their two-year-old daughter, thanks to the efforts of IVF and a donor egg. She had her daddy's brown eyes and a cute little nose that obviously came from her genetic mother, but she was what Cole affectionately called "her mama's girl."

If all went well, their new son would arrive in February, also courtesy of the same medical technology that had brought them Alison.

"Sorry," her son said, lowering his voice. "What time will Grandma and Grandpa get here?"

"Anytime now," Sara answered.

"I'm gonna watch for them." He raced off just as Cole walked in, his cheeks as rosy as his son's from the cold.

"Where's he going so fast?"

"To the living room and his lookout post. My folks should arrive any minute," she reminded him, "and you know Brody. He has to be the first one to spot them."

He snagged a celery stick from the vegetable tray on the counter. "Alison?"

"She's sleeping."

Cole grinned as he threaded his arms around what once had been her waist. "Then we're alone?"

"For the moment, yes."

"And Junior's behaving himself?"

She rubbed the bump in front of her. "He's quiet right now."

"Good, because I want to kiss my wife in private."

In the background, Sara heard Brody squeal with excitement. "You'd better hurry because we're about to get company," she warned.

"Now, Sara. Some things are simply not meant to be rushed."

Sara smiled at her husband. "I couldn't agree more."

* * * * *

Mills & Boon® Large Print Medical

June

July

August

Mills & Boon® Large Print Medical

September

FALLING FOR THE SHEIKH SHE SHOULDN'T	Fiona McArthur
DR CINDERELLA'S MIDNIGHT FLING	Kate Hardy
BROUGHT TOGETHER BY BABY	Margaret McDonagh
ONE MONTH TO BECOME A MUM	Louisa George
SYDNEY HARBOUR HOSPITAL: LUCA'S BAD GIRL	Amy Andrews
THE FIREBRAND WHO UNLOCKED HIS HEART	Anne Fraser

October

GEORGIE'S BIG GREEK WEDDING?	Emily Forbes
THE NURSE'S NOT-SO-SECRET SCANDAL	Wendy S. Marcus
DR RIGHT ALL ALONG	Joanna Neil
SUMMER WITH A FRENCH SURGEON	Margaret Barker
SYDNEY HARBOUR HOSPITAL: TOM'S REDEMPTION	Fiona Lowe
DOCTOR ON HER DOORSTEP	Annie Claydon

November

SYDNEY HARBOUR HOSPITAL: LEXI'S SECRET	Melanie Milburne
WEST WING TO MATERNITY WING!	Scarlet Wilson
DIAMOND RING FOR THE ICE QUEEN	Lucy Clark
NO.1 DAD IN TEXAS	Dianne Drake
THE DANGERS OF DATING YOUR BOSS	Sue MacKay
THE DOCTOR, HIS DAUGHTER AND ME	Leonie Knight